Too Late 2 Apologize

Paid in Pain

By
Davonte 'Lite' Adams

Davonte 'Lite' Adams

COPYRIGHT

TABLE OF CONTENTS

ACKNOWLEDGMENTS

First and foremost, all praise is due to the Most High—Allah—for granting me the willpower, clarity, and strength to bring this project to life. Without divine guidance, none of this would be possible.

To my mother, Cynthia Adams: words can't fully express how much of an inspiration you are to me. Your wisdom, strength, and faith have kept me grounded through life's hardships. You've always believed in me, encouraged me, and pushed me to be great. I hope this book makes you proud. I love you to the moon and back.

To my pops—Big Lite, the original—haha. It's safe to say I did it, Pops! Thank you for always giving me that extra push when I felt like giving up or procrastinating. You believed in this book from the moment I shared the idea, and you told me I could be one of the illest to do it. Now it's time to show the world. I'm grateful for your support, your wisdom, and all the jewels you passed down. Much love, respect, and peace to you.

To my brothers and sisters—Mel, Niasia, Marquis, Nyasia, Rymel, Tifha, and Truss—I got us if nobody else does. Always.

To my uncles—Miz, Sha, and Freddy—special shout out to Miz and Sha for being part of the reason I ever considered becoming an author. And to my auntie Nay Nay, who's also an author—I read all you guys books as a kid, watching, learning, and soaking up game. Don't be surprised if you see pieces of yourselves in this story. (Lol) I gotta give flowers to the GOATs who paved the way.

Davonte 'Lite' Adams

To my aunties—long live Aunt Lorraine, we love and miss you deeply. May Allah be pleased with you. Aunt Michelle, Aunt Nay Nay, Aunt Niecy, Aunt Deck, Aunt Gina. And to my uncles—Uncle Derry and Uncle Trey.

To all my cousins—there are too many to name, but I'll try. 2Live, what up. Keem (I hope this book reaches you), Steven, Destiny, Amaru, Shakira, Brooklyn (Tootie), Quincy, Rick, Precious, Shaniya, Omarion, Bang, Twan, Najae, Daquan, Tahj, Ashleigh, Blinacc (What's Ginood? LMAO). Free Dapp—you'll be home soon, buzzin'. Yogi, Autumn.

To my nieces and nephews—Lanay, Jayla, Daquan, Adrian, DJ (Donald Jr.), Little Rymel, Ariyah, Taleeya, and Rell Rell.

Long live those who are no longer with us—Grandma Dot (we all miss you dearly—may Allah be pleased with you), Derae, David, Uncle John, Phat Man, Mayra, and Shaborn. May God be pleased with you all.

To my grandfather, Alfred Adams—love you, Granddad.

To my friends—thank you for your love and support throughout this journey. Kayri, Bingi, Doug, Chapo, J, T-Macc. My twin Kiwi (hold your head, God got you), Shay (my sons mother), Derria, Leshae, Shawn, Demarcus, Keyasha (thank you for pushing me and believing in me). Dot, Awol, Duney and Binky (hold your heads high, y'all coming home soon), Resa (thanks for the input and support), Speed, Za, T-Money, Luck, Marco, Naz, Ree, Boo-Boo, Yaya (you believed in me before I believed in myself—much love). Rich, Bam (I'm proud of you, ahk), Ea, Melo, Puffy, Kareem, Brick (keep fighting), Ye', Sticky (keep climbing, bro), Fifi, Leggs, Sosa, ink'd by tay, Skooda, Amber, Destiny (thanks for the feedback and support), Teasey, Dc, Ms.Sisk (Your words will forever stick with me. Thank you for everything), Carleasha, Mexico (I'm still waiting on you, you know what time it is), Hakeem, Dank, Tall, Ralo, Solid Kay, Jay Rock, Ishmael, Lil

Donald, Toxic, Basir, Mal, Raqib, Bilal, Squeeze, Quez, Say No More (big shout out to you for helping me finish this project—even when I was a pain in the ass! LMAO).

If you're looking to publish, hit up coldheartedpublications@gmail.com—my bro will get you right, no question.

And last but never least, to my twin, my one and only son, Nehemiah—this is for us, baby boy. I love you more than words could ever describe.

Long live my dawg Paul—you are never forgotten.

To all my supporters—thank you. I appreciate each and every one of you. Stay tuned—there's more coming.

DEDICATION

This novel is dedicated to my beloved grandmother, Dorothy "Dot" Adams. Your presence is deeply missed by the entire family. I know you're looking down with pride. May God be pleased with you.

CHAPTER 1: AFTER SCHOOL RIDE

"Ayo, Blizz, you coming to my crib after school? I got that new 2K that just dropped," Vaughn said, stepping onto the school bus.

"Yeah, we can do that, lil' cuz. I'll bust your ass a few times," Blizz joked.

School had just let out, and the bus was wild. Kids were standing in their seats, tossing paper, shouting over each other. The air smelled like sweat, cheap cologne, and whatever mystery food somebody had stuffed in their backpack over the weekend. Vaughn was in ninth grade, Blizz in tenth. They weren't real cousins, but they told everyone they were. Vaughn looked up to Blizz like a big brother—like the brother he never had.

As he made his way toward the back, he spotted Psalm sitting by the window, scrolling on her phone. She had one foot propped up on the seat, hoodie pulled over her head, AirPods in. She looked unbothered, untouchable, like she didn't give a fuck about anything—but Vaughn knew better.

Psalm was tough, yeah, but her armor had cracks. If you looked close enough, you could see them.

He slid into the seat next to her without hesitation.

"Wassup, Psalm?"

She barely looked up. "Hey, Devaughn."

1

Vaughn groaned. "What I tell you about calling me that? It's Vaughn Smooth, baby."

Psalm scoffed. "You ain't smooth." She tucked her phone into her hoodie pocket and gave him a sideways look. "And get your arm off me—you already know I got a boyfriend."

Vaughn smirked. "And? I got a test tomorrow."

Psalm frowned. "And what does you having a test got to do with anything?"

"Oh, I just thought we was naming shit we was gonna cheat on."

She tried not to, but a laugh slipped out. She turned toward the window, hiding her smile. "Still don't think I'm smooth?" Vaughn pressed, inching closer.

Psalm rolled her eyes. "Boy, if you don't back up—"

But her voice wasn't as sharp as before.

Truth was, she liked this game—the back-and-forth, the attention. She'd never admit it, though. Not out loud. Not when Vaughn had a rep for being a player, always chasing the next girl like it was a sport.

She wasn't trying to be another name on his list.

***

"Ayo, Vaughn, come back here, bro!" Blizz called from the back of the bus. "This nigga Lonnie swear he can fuck with you in a rap battle."

Vaughn sighed. "Aight, cuz, hold on real quick."

He started to stand, but before he could move, a shadow fell over him.

Sada.

"Yo, Psalm, you need to drop that zero and get with this hero," Sada sneered, gripping the back of the seat. His voice carried that usual cocky arrogance. "This bitch-ass, pretty-boy ass nigga bothering you? 'Cause I'll slap this nigga head to the back of the bus if he is."

Psalm tensed. She hated Sada.

Not just because he was a bully, but because he was the type of dude that didn't hear 'no'. He was the type that acted like a girl was playing hard to get when she was really just trying to get away.

And he stayed on her. Always trying to press up, always testing her patience.

She sighed, already exhausted. "Both of y'all getting on my nerves." She nudged Vaughn. "Can I have my seat back, thank you?"

Vaughn stood up, but before he could step away, Sada smacked him in the back of the head. Laughter erupted around them.

Psalm exhaled through her nose. She saw the way Vaughn froze—the way his hands curled into fists, his breathing slowed.

Sada didn't know what he just did.

"Put your hands on me again and watch what happens," Vaughn said through gritted teeth.

Sada smirked. "What you gon' do, little bitch?" He stepped closer, chest puffed out, his massive frame blocking the aisle.

Before Vaughn could react, Blizz was already between them. "Hey, hey, hey— What's the problem?"

Sada didn't take his eyes off Vaughn. "Ain't no problem. But you better get your lil' cousin, your lil' sister, whatever the fuck he is to you, up out my face before I rock his little ass to sleep."

Psalm clenched her jaw.

She didn't want to admit it, but she respected Vaughn for standing his ground. Most dudes let Sada do whatever the fuck he wanted.

But Vaughn? He wasn't built like that. And she kinda liked it.

***

When the bus finally reached their stop, Vaughn stopped at her seat.

"I got something for you," he said, digging in his pocket. He pulled out a bracelet with a small red heart pendant attached.

"I won this at the school pep rally today. I'm giving you my heart—take care of it, you heard?" Psalm looked at him, her face unreadable.
At first, she wanted to clown him. Say some slick shit. But then she saw the way he was looking at her—all cocky on the outside, but underneath that, something real.

She hesitated, then took the bracelet, turning it over in her hand. "…It's cute," she muttered.

4

Vaughn smirked. "I know."

She shook her head. "Boy, get outta here."

But as he walked away, she slid the bracelet onto her wrist.

***

As the bus rolled on, Psalm rested her arm against the window, twisting the bracelet between her fingers.

She wasn't stupid. She knew Vaughn was a flirt. But still… A small smile ghosted across her lips.

Maybe he wasn't as smooth as he thought.

But he was getting there.

***

As they walked home, Vaughn finally spoke.

"Yo, son… I'ma fuck Psalm real soon, watch."

Blizz shook his head, laughing. "Man, I don't even know why you like that girl so much. She mean as fuck, and she slick be dressing like a tomboy or something. Like, what's up with that?"

"Man, you gotta look past all that," Vaughn said. "She really is beautiful. She just a lil rough around the edges. But I'ma bring that sexy out of her, watch."

Blizz laughed harder. "Man, she got you wide open."

They turned the corner onto Vaughn's block. That's when he saw it. A bright orange paper taped to his front door.

His stomach dropped.

"The fuck is this on my door?"

He stepped up to the porch, snatched it down. His eyes scanned the words, and a sick feeling twisted in his chest.

Eviction Notice.

His fingers tightened around the paper. The words blurred. Three days. That's all they had.

His mind raced. Things where hard enough as it was, where was he going to get the money from.

He turned to Blizz, his voice low. "Yo…"

Blizz glanced at the paper. His face fell.

"What the fuck we gon' do?" Vaughn whispered.

CHAPTER 2: A HARSH AWAKENING

Beep. Beep. Beep.

Vaughn rolled over and silenced the alarm. 7:30 AM.

A deep sigh left his lips. Today was supposed to be a big day—the annual Hempstead block party, the biggest event of the summer. Everybody who was somebody was going to be there.

Sliding out of bed, he grabbed a pre-rolled blunt from the nightstand and lit it up. The first hit rushed to his lungs, settling the tension in his chest. He leaned back and exhaled slow, watching the smoke swirl toward the ceiling.

Reaching for the remote, he turned up the music.

NBA YoungBoy's "Fuck the Industry" blasted through the speakers, the bass shaking the walls.

Vaughn smirked as he pulled his fresh fit from the closet— Amiri jeans, a clean-ass Amiri tee, and crisp white Air Forces.

"Oh yeah, I'm about to be the cleanest nigga at the party tonight," he muttered, setting up the iron.

Then—Devaughn!! Devaughn!!"

His mother's voice cut through the music.

"What, Ma?!" he called back, barely paying attention.

The door swung open.

7

Dee Dee stepped inside, scratching at her neck—a telltale sign of her addiction.

"Hey, baby… why don't you go on and hook your mama up with a wake-up?" she said, her voice smooth but desperate.

Vaughn clenched his jaw.

His mother—the woman he once looked up to as his queen, his protector, his superwoman—was nothing but a ghost of who she used to be. Strung out. Lost. Addicted.

He hated this reality, but it was his reality.

And yeah, he sold crack to his own mother.

At least if she was gonna buy, the money was going into his pocket—to put food in the fridge, keep the lights on, and hold shit down.

But seeing her like this? Begging for another hit?

That shit stung.

"Man, hell naw. What happened to the money I gave you to go pay the rent?" Vaughn snapped. Dee Dee shifted her weight, fingers twitching, eyes darting around the room.

"Baby, I was on my way, I swear! But—" she sighed, clutching her chest like she was heartbroken—"you ain't gon' believe what happened. When I stopped at the store, these two boys ran up on me and snatched my purse!"

Vaughn's fists tightened around the iron. She was lying.
Nobody was robbing crackheads in the hood. Plus, he had seen that same damn purse sitting on her nightstand last night.

"Oh yeah?" he said, his tone dripping in sarcasm. "That's crazy… 'cause we just got these eviction papers, and I got three days to come up with sixteen hundred dollars."

He spoke while pressing out the wrinkles in his Amiri jeans. Vaughn stayed fly—no matter what was happening around him.

Dee Dee sighed. "Well, shit, Devaughn… I got six dollars! Give me something, goddamn." Vaughn grabbed the six bucks, slid it into his pocket, then handed her a small baggie.
"Here, man. Now let me finish getting dressed."

Dee Dee snatched it and ran out of the room faster than a kid playing tag.

Vaughn shook his head. Same shit, different day.

***

Before heading out, Vaughn peeked into his little sister's room.

Jewel—just twelve years old—was the only light in his dark world.

She could do no wrong in his eyes.

She sat cross-legged on the floor, coloring on a big-ass poster board. When she saw him, her face lit up.

"Hey, baby girl, what you doing?" Vaughn asked, his voice softer.

"Nothing, just coloring this poster for my project at school. Look!" She held up her drawing.

9

A stick-figure sketch of her and Vaughn, standing in front of a big house with a dog.

Vaughn's throat tightened.

"It's beautiful, princess," he said, crouching down beside her. "One day, I'm gonna make this picture come to life, okay?"

Jewel nodded, smiling. "Okay!"

Vaughn ruffled her hair. "Alright, princess, I'm out. I'll see you later, aight?" As he reached the door—"Vaughn!"

He turned. "Yeah, princess?"

She beamed. "You're the best brother. I love you." His heart melted.

"I love you too, princess."

***

Stepping outside, Vaughn walked down a few houses to Blizz's crib. He picked up a rock and launched it at the window.

A few seconds later, Blizz's head popped out.

"Here I come, bro! Give me a minute!"

Vaughn nodded, pulling out his phone.

He had messages from a few girls trying to link up. But one unread text caught his attention. Omega.
"Call me ASAP. I need you to do me a favor."

Vaughn's stomach dropped.

What type of favor does this nigga want from me?

He dialed.

A deep voice answered.

"Wassup, Omega? You said to give you a call."

"Waddup, Vaughn? How everything going with you?"

"Man, not too good, bro. I gotta come up with this rent money, or I'ma get evicted in three days." Omega paused.
"Damn, lil' homie. That's crazy. I ain't doing too good either, but I might got a solution. I could help you… if you help me."

Vaughn frowned. "What kinda favor?"

"You remember Ronnie, right?"

Vaughn's expression darkened. "Ya man Ronnie with the white Beamer?"

"Yeah… well, he ain't my man no more. Word is, he got knocked with a brick of white… and he's cooperating with the feds."

Silence.

"I need him gone. Like yesterday."

Vaughn swallowed hard. "Yo, Omega, I hear you… but I ain't no killer."

"I know you ain't," Omega said. "But your cousin Blizz? Word is, he gets busy." Vaughn's mouth went dry.

"Man, I don't know, Omega. I gotta holla at him first."

Omega chuckled. "Check your Cash App."

Vaughn glanced at his phone.

$5,000 deposit.

"That's five racks," Omega said. "You'll get the other five when the job's done. Ronnie'll be at the block party tonight."

Click.

The line went dead.

Vaughn stared at his phone.

"Yo, who was that?" Blizz asked, stepping outside.

Vaughn forced a smirk.

"Oh, just this lil' chick I met. She want a nigga to come beat her back in again tonight." Blizz laughed. "Boy, you got too many hoes."

Vaughn chuckled—but his mind was elsewhere.

Ten thousand dollars.

Could he really do this?

Tonight... everything was about to change.

***

As they walked around to the side of the house, Vaughn's mind was racing.

He had three days before they got put out. Three days before his little sister, Jewel, had to pack her shit and sleep God-knows-where.

Three days before he lost everything.

Blizz paused by the brick wall near his house and knelt down. "Hold up, let me grab my baby real quick."
Vaughn watched as Blizz pulled a loose brick from the wall, reached inside, and came back up holding a black Glock 40.

The metal gleamed in the sunlight, almost like it was grinning at him.

Vaughn swallowed hard.

Blizz looked up, noticing him staring.

"Don't watch me, nigga. Look out—make sure nobody see me."

Vaughn turned his back, scanning the street, his heart thudding against his ribs. Behind him, he heard Blizz blow dust off the Glock, checking the clip.
"Aight, we good," Blizz muttered, tucking the gun into his waistband.

Vaughn turned around slowly.

His chest felt tight. His palms sweaty.

13

Blizz saw it all over his face.

"Yo, man, why you always gotta bring that shit everywhere we go?" Vaughn asked, trying to keep his voice steady.

Blizz locked eyes with him. "'Cause, nigga… it get crazy out here." His tone was sharp. "And I'll be damned if my moms gotta bury me before I bury her."

He adjusted his hoodie.

"And I ain't tryna see you in no casket neither, my nigga." Vaughn nodded, but his throat felt dry.

Blizz tilted his head. "What's up with you?"

Vaughn exhaled.

This was it. The moment he had to make a choice. "I need one."
Blizz chuckled, shaking his head. "Man, you don't need no gun. I'ma hold us down with this muthafucka right here." He patted his waistband.

Vaughn didn't laugh.

He stepped closer. "I'm serious, bro. I need one."

Blizz's smirk faded.

He studied Vaughn's face—saw the look in his eyes.

This wasn't a joke.

This wasn't just about self-defense.

Blizz let out a slow breath, then nodded.

"Aight," he said, voice low. "Let's go to my people's and get you one then."

He tucked his hoodie over his Glock and started walking.

Vaughn followed.

Each step felt heavier than the last.

CHAPTER 3: STREETS ON FIRE

"Damn, son, the block is lit," Blizz said, passing the Backwood to Vaughn.

"Yeah, it is," Vaughn replied, taking a deep pull as they sat on the cherry-red Camaro. They had peeled the car earlier that day—had to pull up to the block party in style.
The DJ had the whole block jumping. Music boomed through massive speakers, bass rattling windows. The streets were packed.

Gamblers shot cee-lo against the wall, while the big-time hustlers smoked and laughed. Gold diggers and hoodrats roamed in packs, looking for their next come-up.

Everybody and their mama was outside.

Vaughn was fresh as hell, his diamond-studded chain glistened under the streetlights, reflecting off his Rolex and earrings.

Slim with a light complexion, a fade haircut curling at the top, and striking green eyes, he always figured he had a little Hispanic or white in his blood.

Blizz, on the other hand, had a rougher look—brown-skinned, a unibrow, and a chipped front tooth. He always kept a mug on his face, not because he was mad, but because he didn't like smiling too much.

Still, he was a real one.

A group of girls passed, eyeing them.

"Hey Blizz, hey Vaughn! Nice car."

"Good lookin', ma," Blizz replied smoothly.

Vaughn smirked, eyeing one of the girls. "Damn, that ass fat," he muttered.

Blizz exhaled, taking another pull. "Yo, I'ma tear a bitch up tonight," he said, popping a Percocet into his mouth and swallowing it dry.

Vaughn side-eyed him. "You and these percs, man. You need to slow down on them muhfuckas."

He smoked occasionally, but he didn't fuck with pills.

"Nah, fuck that. These shits keep me on point," Blizz muttered, nodding toward the other side of the street.

"Like right now—look at Sada and his punk-ass crew, eyeing us."

Vaughn looked up.

Across the street, Sada and his boys stood, arms crossed, staring hard. They locked eyes for a moment—a silent standoff. Then, Sada and his crew kept it moving.

Blizz gripped the hammer at his waist. "We gon' get that fat-head ass nigga." Vaughn nodded, pulling out his phone.
As he checked his messages, Psalm walked by with her girls.

Without thinking, he reached out and grabbed her wrist.

***

"Where you going, beautiful?"

Psalm froze. Her homegirls paused, watching.

"What's up, ladies?" Blizz added, his voice smooth.

"Just walking around. Now, can you let my arm go?" Psalm said, raising an eyebrow. Vaughn smirked. "How about you chill with me for a second? Help me finish this Backwood." She hesitated. "I don't know…"
"It's fine, ma. We ain't doing nothing but chilling."

Finally, she took the blunt, inhaled deeply, and exhaled slowly.

"Nice car," she said.

"It'd look even better with you in the front seat," Vaughn grinned.

"Boy, please. I know what you and Blizz be up to. Y'all ain't no good," she teased.

"And you got too many bitches. I ain't about to have no hoes checking me over you."

"Man, fuck them hoes. I'd drop all of them just to be with you," Vaughn said, inching closer. Psalm almost believed him— until she snapped back to reality.
"That's too bad, Vaughn. I'm taken. Plus, I've known you since sixth grade."

Vaughn smirked. "Man, fuck that cornball-ass nigga. He not even your type."

"How you figure?"

"I can tell by the way you look at me. Plus… you wearing my heart on your sleeve."

He nodded at her wrist.

The bracelet he gave her was still there.

She smiled.

Then—"Psalm! Psalm! Girl, you better get right—there go Jetson!"

Her eyes widened.

Jetson was already walking toward them.

His face twisted in anger.

"What the fuck is you doing?" Jetson barked.

Psalm quickly stepped back. "Nothing, baby! We was just chilling and smoking!" Jetson's eyes burned into Vaughn.
Vaughn smirked—then did something reckless.

He slid his arm around Psalm's waist.

"Yeah, we was just smoking, right baby?"

Then he planted a sloppy kiss on her neck.

Jetson saw red.

"Bitch, let's fucking GO!" He snatched Psalm's arm, dragging her away.

Vaughn watched, shaking his head.

"Bitch-ass nigga."

Psalm's homegirls stared him down.

"Now you know you dead wrong for that, Vaughn."

He ignored them, checking his phone.

A new text.

Meanwhile, Blizz was pouring liquor down some chick's throat, laughing.

"Yo, Blizz, I got a sale up the block. I'ma be right back."

"Aight, fam." Blizz said, still laughing.

Vaughn disappeared down the block, his mind locked on the job he had to do.

Ahead, Ronnie stood leaning against his cocaine-white BMW M5, a New York fitted pulled low over his eyes.

A bad little Puerto Rican chick was hugged up next to him, her thick thighs poured into tight blue jean shorts. She was stroking his ego, laughing at everything he said while he sipped on a bottle of Remy.

"Hell yeah, ma, I paid fifty racks cash for this muhfucka right here. Pink slip and all," Ronnie bragged.

"Oh yeah?" she purred, trailing her fingers over his diamond chain.

Ronnie smirked. "No doubt. I get money on the daily, baby. Ain't no lil' boy shit with me."

He leaned in, whispering, "Matter fact, let's hop in this fast motherfucker and slide to my spot." She giggled, licking her lips. "Lemme just tell my homegirl real quick."

Ronnie nodded. "Aight, hurry that ass up."

He watched her hips sway as she walked away, already plotting his next move.

"Hell yeah, I'm 'bout to tear that ass up tonight," he muttered, hitting the bottle again.

He checked his Rolex—didn't even notice Vaughn walking up behind him.

"Yo, whaddup, Ronnie?"

Ronnie turned, slightly squinting.

"It's me, Vaughn. From Wyandanch."

Recognition flickered.

"Oh yeah… lil' dude from up the block. Be getting his hustle on at the store."

"What's up, young blood?" Ronnie dapped him up.

"Shit, my nigga, I'm just out here tryna get it, you feel me? Tryna make every dollar count." Ronnie nodded. "Most definitely. Young nigga, get that money by any means."

Vaughn smirked. "No doubt you eating, big homie. That's why I'm tryna fuck with you."

Ronnie took another sip. "Oh yeah?"

"Yeah. I got some trash-ass coke from my connect, son. Can't do nothing with it. I was hoping you could throw me a O or two, big homie."

Ronnie chuckled. "Nah, son, I don't front shit."

Vaughn shook his head. "Nah, I ain't asking for a front, big bro. I'm tryna spend bread." He pulled out a stack of blue hundreds—$4,000 cash.

Ronnie's eyebrows raised slightly.

This young nigga had to be stupid—or desperate.

"Naw, lil' homie. I ain't got it."

Ronnie turned his attention back to the party, scanning for his shorty.

But Vaughn wasn't letting up.

"Come on, big bro, fuck with me. How you gon' tell me to stay hungry, but you ain't tryna feed me?"

He pulled out the cash again, trying to hand it over.

Ronnie waved it off. "Ayo, don't hand me that shit out here!"

He lowered his voice. "Lil' nigga, put that bread up. I'ma serve you, but not right here." He nodded toward the space between two houses.

"Come on. Let's walk."

Vaughn nodded. "Aight, cool."

He kept it smooth, playing his role.

But his heart was pounding.

This was it.

***

They stepped into the dark alleyway.

Ronnie crept up behind Vaughn, thinking fast.

This young nigga green as fuck.

I'ma just choke his lil' ass out and take that $4,000. They moved deeper into the shadows.

Ronnie flexed his fingers, getting ready.

Then—Vaughn stopped suddenly.

"You know what, Ronnie?"

Ronnie hesitated.

"Yeah?"

Before he could move—Vaughn spun around—Glock aimed straight at his forehead. "I can't stand a rat."

Ronnie's face drained of color.

"Woah, woah! Hold on, baby! I—I ain't no rat, young blood. Go—goo, gone ahead and drop that gun before you hurt somebody, lil' homie."

Ronnie's hands were shaking.

Vaughn's grip tightened.

"Naw. It's 'bout time I drop you."

His finger wrapped around the trigger.

This was it.

He was about to get his stripes.

Omega was gonna fuck with him heavy now.

And most importantly—he had to pay the rent for Jewel.

She was depending on him.

Vaughn clenched his teeth.

Ronnie closed his eyes, bracing himself.

"Omega sends his regards." Said Vaughn. Preparing to send him to his maker.

Then—"Yeah, wassup now, little pussy?! You ain't got your cousin to save you now!"

Vaughn's head snapped up.

At the other end of the alley, Sada and his crew stood, blocking his escape. **Vaughn turned for half a second—** just enough time for Ronnie to see his chance. BAM!

Ronnie kicked Vaughn dead in the nuts—hard as fuck.

"UGHHH!"

Vaughn crumpled to the ground, his Glock clattering onto the pavement.

Ronnie took off running.

Vaughn gritted his teeth, grabbed the gun, and jumped up.

His vision blurred with pain—but he wasn't letting Ronnie get away.

BANG! BANG!

He let off two shots.

Ronnie ducked, sprinting toward his car.

BANG! BANG! BANG!

Vaughn emptied the clip.

One bullet caught Ronnie in the right shoulder.

He stumbled forward but managed to yank open his car door.

The block erupted into chaos.

People screamed, ran, ducked behind cars.

Ronnie threw himself into the driver's seat, his hoodie soaking in blood.

He pressed start—the Beamer roared to life.

Tires squealed as he peeled off, swerving through the crowd.

"Fuck, I'm hit. I can't believe I'm hit!"

Ronnie gritted his teeth, fishing for his phone.

His fingers trembled as he typed.

He found the number he needed and sent a desperate text:

"I've been shot. Omega knows I'm working with y'all. He tried to kill me. You gotta help me!"

He dropped the phone, panting hard.

His vision blurred.

He swerved onto an empty street—finally safe.

Then—his stomach dropped.

His eyes widened in horror.

In the rearview mirror…

A pair of cold, dark eyes stared back at him.

Then—He felt it.

The cold steel of a gun barrel against his temple.

A voice whispered.

"You can let me out right here, my mans."

BOOM!

Blood splattered the driver's side window.

The car jerked forward.

The horn blared through the night.

A shadow moved in the back seat.

Blizz slid out, wiped his face, and disappeared into the darkness.

CHAPTER 4: SHADOWS OF DECEIT

The yellow crime scene tape fluttered in the late-night breeze as Detective Grayson and Detective Vega ducked under it.

Flashing red and blue lights bathed the block in a chaotic glow, illuminating the lifeless body slumped in the front seat of a white BMW.

A rookie officer hurried over, sweat beading at his hairline, clutching a small notepad.

"From the evidence, it looks like a clean execution. One gunshot wound to the back of the head. The shooter was likely in the back seat. It wasn't a robbery—the victim's money, phone, and jewelry are untouched. We found a .40 caliber shell casing. Someone wanted this guy gone."

Detective Grayson took a long, slow drag of his Newport, the tip glowing red in the darkness. Then—without warning—he exhaled the smoke directly into the rookie's face.
The rookie coughed, eyes watering.

Grayson smirked, flicking his cigarette to the pavement before grinding it out with his expensive Stacey Adams loafers.

"Any witnesses?" he asked, his tone laced with condescension.

The rookie shifted uncomfortably, lowering his voice. "Uh, we got one potential witness. When we arrived, he was walking down the block, away from the vehicle. He's in patrol car six. We haven't questioned him yet because—"

"Hey, kid," Grayson cut him off, rolling his neck lazily.

The rookie swallowed. "Yes, sir?"

"You ever been told you talk too fucking much?"

The rookie's face flushed red. He quickly shut his mouth.

Without another word, Grayson and Vega walked off toward the patrol car.

***

The two detectives were infamous in Nassau County—not for their dedication to justice, but for being the dirtiest cops on the force. Probably the dirtiest cops in the whole state of New York.

They didn't solve crimes.

They manipulated them.

They played by their own rules, and everyone in the streets knew it.

And tonight was no different.

Inside patrol car six, a loud, aggressive voice echoed through the vehicle.

"I'm innocent, you bitch-ass pigs! Let me the fuck go! I want my lawyer, motherfucker!" Detective Grayson smirked.
Sada.

The back door swung open, revealing the handcuffed suspect.

Sweat glistened off Sada forehead, his wide chest rising and falling, his eyes wild with fury. As soon as he saw Grayson, he sneered.

"And who the fuck are you supposed to be, you spaghetti-eating motherfucker?"

Grayson chuckled, leaning in close.

Then—without warning—his hand shot out, clamping around Sada's thick throat.

Sada's eyes bulged, his breath cut off as his face turned purple.

"Now listen up, you fat piece of shit," Grayson hissed, his breath reeked of cigarettes and power trips.

"You're gonna shut the fuck up and tell me what I want to hear."

Sada gasped, his lungs begging for air.

Grayson tightened his grip.

"Who did Omega send for this hit?"

He finally released him, and Sada collapsed forward, coughing violently. Drool dripped from his mouth as he struggled to catch his breath.

"I don't know, man!" he wheezed. "I was just walking home!"

Wrong answer.

Grayson's fist slammed into Sada gut, knocking the wind out of him. Sada doubled over, vomiting on himself.

Grayson sighed, shaking his head.

"Try again, fat boy."

He yanked Sada out of the car, dragging him face-first against the trunk before patting him down.

"Fuck you, man! I know my rights!" Sada choked out.

Grayson smirked, reaching into his own pocket.

Then, smooth as silk, he slipped a small bag of cocaine into Sada's jacket. "Yeah?" he muttered. "Well, fuck your rights."
He snapped his fingers.

"Search him for weapons or narcotics."

The rookie officer rushed over, his hands trembling as he dug into Sada's pockets. Moments later, he pulled out the planted cocaine.
"Well, well, what do we have here?" the rookie said.

Sada face twisted in fury.

"Man, he planted that shit on me! Dirty-ass motherfucking cop! That's his shit!" Grayson rolled his eyes.
"Yeah, yeah. Tell it to the judge, chubby."

He shoved Sada back into the cruiser.

"Take him downtown," he ordered before dusting off his hands and walking away.

***

Detective Vega was a few feet away, speaking with an EMS worker as they tried to calm down a hysterical young woman.

Grayson barely paid attention at first—another grieving relative losing it over a body.

But then he noticed the way she was hyperventilating, her entire body trembling uncontrollably. She was in full-blown panic attack mode, gasping for breath between gut-wrenching sobs.

One of the paramedics crouched beside her, his voice calm but firm.

"Miss, I need you to try and take a deep breath. Can you tell me your full name?"

The young woman's breath hitched in her throat, and for a moment, she struggled to speak. Then, through ragged, shallow gasps, she choked out:

"Psalm Rivera..."

Grayson's cigarette burned between his fingers, but he wasn't listening.

Vega barely glanced in their direction.

To them, she was just another mourning niece, another piece in the puzzle of this murder. But Psalm was Ronnie's niece.

And just like that, the weight of the murder hits differently.

CHAPTER 5: BLOOD, BRICKS, & BETRAYAL

"Grrp, grrp, grrp—oh, shit, ma," Vaughn sighed in pleasure as he lounged in his midnight black 550 Benz, getting topped off by Astoria, a neighborhood shorty with a mouth like magic.

"Grrp, grrp," was the sound she made as she deep-throated him, her glossy lips working him over.

"Baby, my jaws hurt," she gasped, coming up for air, wiping her mouth.

"Keep going, ma. That shit feel good," Vaughn groaned, gripping the back of her head and guiding her back down.

His iPhone vibrated in the cupholder. He snatched it up, seeing Omega's name flash across the screen.

He answered lazily, "Yo."

"Hello, my friend. How are you?" Omega's deep accent came through the line.

"Everything is everything, my man. What's good?" Vaughn replied, exhaling smoke.

"Business as usual. I want you to come to my residence— you and your friend, Blizz. I want to talk business and thank you both," Omega said smoothly.

"Aight, bet. Give me about an hour—"

"I don't have an hour to spare, my friend. Come now."

Click. The line went dead.

Vaughn tossed his phone back into the cupholder.

"Yo, shorty, watch out. I gotta slide," he said, nudging Astoria off him.

She wiped her mouth, looking up at him. "Are you at least dropping me home? And what about dinner tonight? You promised."

"Nah, baby, I can't drop you right now. You gon' have to walk or call an Uber or something. And tonight? I'ma be busy. We gon' have to reschedule."

Astoria folded her arms, lips pressed in disbelief. "I can't believe you right now, Vaughn."

Vaughn leaned over, popped open her door. "I'ma make it up to you, love." Then, without another word, he pushed her out and peeled off, leaving her standing there, dumbfounded.

As he sped off, he dialed Blizz.

"Yo," Blizz answered.

"What's good? Omega want us to pull up to his crib. He gotta talk business." "Say that. I'm at the spot, come scoop me," Blizz said.

"Bet. Be there in ten." Vaughn hung up and stepped on the gas, heading straight for Blizz's house.

***

It had been a week since the block party murder. Everything had cooled down.

No names were being mentioned. No heat was coming their way. The police didn't have a clue who was responsible.

Omega sent the remaining five racks, plus an extra five, for handling business. Vaughn and Blizz split the money down the middle—Vaughn used his half to cover rent and copped himself a fresh Cherry red 550 Benz.

Money was about to start flowing big, and they were ready to take off.

Vaughn pulled up to Blizz's house and beeped the horn. Moments later, Blizz jogged out and hopped in.

"Yo, what's good, bro?" Blizz said, dapping him up.

"Shit, just chillin', my nigga," Vaughn replied, pulling off.

He grabbed a half-smoked blunt from the ashtray, put a flame to it, took a deep pull, and passed it to Blizz.

"Where you coming from, son?" Blizz asked, hitting the blunt.

"Shit, slid through on that bitch Astoria for a minute. Took her to grab some food, then she topped me off in the car. Left her standing on the curb after that," Vaughn said nonchalantly.

Blizz shook his head. "You ain't never give a fuck, man."

"And you know this!" Vaughn laughed, dapping Blizz again.

Blizz stretched his legs out in the Benz. "Matter of fact, since we talking about spits, let me tell you what happened to me the other day."

Vaughn flicked ash out the window. "What happened?"

Blizz smirked, shaking his head. "Yo, listen. I'm at the mall, right? Just left Foot Locker when I peep this bad-ass jawn walking by. I'm talkin' top-tier—yellow bone, short hair, thick in all the right places. Gucci down, looking like money moves on legs."

Vaughn exhaled slow, watching the smoke swirl. "Word?"

"Word. So I shoot my shot, get her number, and before I even get to the car, shorty texts me like, 'Yo, come through right now, I need that.'"

Vaughn side-eyed him. "Nigga, stop lying."

"Swear to God! At first, I'm thinking it's a setup, but I had the .40 on me, so I wasn't sweating it. She sent the Addy, and ten minutes later, I'm knocking on her door."

Vaughn raised a brow. "And?"

"Nigga, soon as I step in, she on me. No talk, no Netflix, just straight to unbuckling my belt." Vaughn smirked. "Damn, shorty was ready."

"Too ready, bro. I lean back, let her do her thing, and I swear on my momma, I ain't never had my dick sucked like that before. It was like she was training for the Olympics."

Vaughn chuckled. "You was living the dream."

Blizz held up a finger. "For a minute, yeah. But then… nigga, shit got crazy." Vaughn frowned. "What happened?"

Blizz sighed like he had PTSD. "So I'm hitting it from the back, right? Everything smooth… until outta nowhere—this smell smack me in the face like a brick wall."

Vaughn twisted his face up. "Nah."

"YES. At first, I thought something was dead in the crib. Like a rat crawled in the vents and died. But then it hit me—it was her."

Vaughn burst out laughing, nearly choking on his smoke. "Nigga, stop playing!"

"I swear! I tried to keep going, thinking my nose was tripping, but nah—the funk got stronger, like spoiled milk mixed with regret."

Vaughn was crying laughing. "Yo, what you do?!"

Blizz exhaled. "I did what any real nigga would do—I spit on her back, acted like I nutted, pulled up my pants, and got the fuck out."

Vaughn lost it. "You a wild nigga, man!"

Blizz shook his head. "Bitch still blowing up my phone, talking 'bout she miss me." Vaughn wiped tears from his eyes as they pulled up to Omega's mansion.

The night had started with laughs.

But inside that mansion, shit was about to get real.

***

The iron gates of Omega's estate creaked open like the doors of a fortress, revealing a mansion straight out of a cartel boss's dream.

Acres of pristine land stretched in every direction. Parked around a massive stone fountain were Bentleys, Maybachs, Lamborghinis, and Ferraris—each one gleaming under golden lights, like trophies of a man who never took a loss.

Two masked gunmen, holding AK-47s, stood statuesque at the front door. Their fingers rested lightly on the triggers—not a threat, just a reminder: nobody moved through here unchecked.

A maid in a sleek black uniform approached, her heels clicking on the stone pavement as she opened the car door.

"Follow me, gentlemen," she said in a smooth, detached voice, leading them inside.

Inside, the mansion was even more opulent—marble floors, million-dollar paintings, and ceilings high enough to make God jealous.

The white walls were untouched by dirt, like sin was only committed in the shadows.

As they passed through the kitchen, Vaughn clocked the naked women in masks at the counter, expertly chopping kilos of pure white powder.

They moved like a well-oiled machine, slicing, packaging, and sealing with military precision.

The maid led them out to the backyard, where Omega lay stretched out on a beach chair, soaking up the sun like a king surveying his empire.

***

"Hola, amigos," Omega greeted, standing up.

At 5'5", Omega was short, but he carried himself like a giant.

His clean-shaven face, slicked-back curly Puerto Rican hair, and all-white linen suit made him look effortless, like he hadn't worried about a thing in years.

"Welcome to mi casa," Omega said, spreading his arms.

"Appreciate that. Thanks for having us," Vaughn said, nodding.

"Of course, amigos. You did good work for me. What's mine is yours—drinks, women, whatever you want. Just say the word."

Blizz grinned, leaning back. "Hell yeah, that light brown jawn in the kitchen with the big-ass titties? Bring her out here. And a bottle of Patron."

Omega chuckled, snapping his fingers. "Done."

Vaughn shot Blizz a death stare. Blizz already knew what that look meant—they weren't here for distractions.

"And you?" Omega asked Vaughn.

Vaughn shook his head. "Nah, I'm good. I appreciate the hospitality, but we here to talk business."

Omega smirked. "Straight to the point. I like that. Sit down, let's talk."

Vaughn leaned forward. "We appreciate all this, but if you really wanna thank us—hit us off with some bricks."

Omega tilted his head, intrigued.

"Bricks? No." He let the answer settle. "You two are corner boys—I give you two ounces a week, max. You can't handle keys."

Vaughn didn't flinch. "That's true, but with Ronnie gone, we can fill his shoes. We're ready to run that territory."

Omega swirled his drink. "Yes, but with territory comes enemies. You two are still teenagers. Still in school."

Vaughn smirked. "We already put in work to show we ain't playing. We'll build a team to move the product so we can re-up faster. And fuck school—we tryna get paid."

Omega studied them, stroking his chin, his expression unreadable.

"This is a dangerous game," Omega said finally. "Once you're in, you're in. You sure you're ready?"

Vaughn's jaw tightened. "Ain't never been more sure of anything." Omega nodded. "Alright. Let me show you something."

Omega led them through the house, down a long hallway, and into the basement. The air was thicker down here, heavy with something unspoken.

A single, flickering light bulb cast eerie shadows against the walls.

In the center of the room, two men sat tied to chairs, blindfolded, mouths gagged. Omega circled them like a predator among prey.

"In this game, you need soldiers. But more than that, you need trust. And trust? That's rare," Omega said, ripping the blindfolds off.

The first man flinched, his eyes wild with fear.

"This one?" Omega mused. "Been stealing from me. Hundreds of thousands."

He drove a fist into the man's gut, making him gag behind the tape. Then, one by one, he bent each of his fingers backward until they snapped like twigs.

The man's muffled screams filled the basement. Then— BANG!

A single bullet to the head silenced him forever.

Blood splattered onto Vaughn's face.

He wiped it off, his heartbeat steady—but something in his stomach twisted.

Omega turned to the second man.

"This one? My most trusted lieutenant. We grew up together."

He sighed. "And yet, he betrayed me."

41

Omega pulled out a switchblade—and sliced half the man's tongue off.

The man screamed, his eyes bulging, body thrashing against the ropes.

Omega handed the gun to Vaughn.

"Now I need to know if I can trust you. Finish him."

Vaughn's palms sweated. His finger hovered over the trigger.

His breath felt heavy, like his chest was full of bricks.

The man pleaded with his eyes.

Vaughn's hands shook.

Then—he lowered the gun.

"I can't do it."

Omega's face darkened with disappointment.

Then—BANG! BANG!

Blizz shoved Vaughn aside and put two shots through the man's forehead.

Blood sprayed the walls like abstract art.

Blizz grinned, licking his lips. "Now, that's how you handle business."

Omega turned to Blizz, a slow smile spreading across his face.

"Now I know who really took out Ronnie," he said, his voice smooth, almost amused.

Blizz grinned, eyes locked on the lifeless body like a wolf fresh off a kill.

Omega shifted his gaze back to Vaughn, reading him like an open book. He placed a firm hand on his shoulder, giving it a reassuring pat.

"It's okay, Vaughn. You haven't had your first one yet," Omega said, his tone understanding—but underneath, there was something else.

A test passed, but not without a mark left behind.

Vaughn exhaled slowly, his fingers still tingling from gripping the trigger.

His stomach felt heavy, like a weight had been dropped inside of him.

Omega stretched his arms.

"That's enough for today," he said, motioning toward the stairs.

The basement air still hung thick with the scent of gunpowder, sweat, and fresh death.

And as Vaughn followed Omega up the steps, he couldn't shake the feeling that a part of him was still sitting in that chair—blindfolded, bound, waiting for his turn.

CHAPTER 6: KEYS TO THE STREETS

Psalm sat at her makeup desk, using a damp rag to wipe off her smudged mascara. She was relieved the funeral was finally over.

Funerals always felt so sad and fake to her—people pretending to grieve, shedding tears for show, only to be laughing and planning food gatherings right after.

The only good thing was seeing a few family members she hadn't seen in a while. Including her mother.

Even though her mother had abandoned her at fourteen.

Psalm's chest tightened at the memory.

Her mother had fallen madly in love with a man she barely knew and moved him into their house. It wasn't long before he convinced her that Psalm was ungrateful and rebellious—that she thought she was grown.

Just like that, her own mother put her out.

That was when life hit Psalm hard.

She bounced between friends' houses, never wanting to feel like a burden. On nights when she had nowhere to go, she broke into cars just to have a warm place to sleep.

Stealing became second nature—not by choice, but by survival. Food. Clothes. Money.

Anything to get by.

But things changed when she met Jetson.

They met during her freshman year, and when he found out about her situation, he moved her in with him and his mother.

Psalm had been grateful.

If it weren't for him, she might still be on the streets.

At first, she loved him—not just for giving her a roof over her head, but because he was sweet, protective.

But over time, she learned that Jetson could be controlling—sometimes even abusive. Still, she stayed.

Yet, lately, she couldn't stop thinking about Vaughn.

She didn't understand why.

When she woke up, he was on her mind.

Before she went to sleep, it was the same.

Even now, as she sat at her makeup desk, her thoughts drifted to him.

A sudden slam of the front door yanked her out of her thoughts.

"Baby! Where you at, girl?"

Jetson's voice boomed through the apartment.

She immediately knew he was drunk—his words slurred, his volume louder than usual. "In the bedroom, babe," she called back.

Seconds later, he stumbled into the room, staggering toward her.

Wrapping his arms around her from behind, he planted a wet kiss on her cheek.

"What's up, baby? How you feelin'?" he murmured into her ear.

His breath reeked of cheap liquor, making her stomach churn.

Psalm clenched her jaw but didn't say anything.

Pointing it out would only piss him off.

And when Jetson was drunk, he got aggressive.

"Honestly, I still don't know how I feel," she admitted, her voice low.

"Uncle Ronnie was like my best friend. I'm just… still in shock that he's gone."

But her words fell on deaf ears.

Jetson started kissing her neck, his hands creeping over her body.

She sighed, knowing exactly where this was going.

He was drunk and horny.

Psalm stood up abruptly, making her way to the bathroom, splashing cold water on her face. But Jetson followed her.

"It's gonna be all right, baby," he said, hugging her from behind again.

This time, his hands roamed, groping her breasts, gripping her ass.

He unbuttoned the top of her pants, his breath hot against her skin.

Psalm stiffened.

She liked sex with him—but not like this.

Not when he was sloppy drunk.

Not when his touch repulsed her instead of exciting her.

She grabbed his hand and pushed him away.

"Not right now, Jetson."

"Don't act like that," he muttered, sliding his hand back down the front of her pants.

She turned around and pressed her palms against his chest, gently pushing him back. "Please, baby. Not right now. I'm really not in the mood."

Jetson's expression darkened.

His arms stretched out, as if she had just insulted him.

"Why the fuck not?"

Psalm swallowed. "I just buried my uncle. I'm just not in the mood, okay?"

He narrowed his eyes, looking her up and down.

"No, it ain't your uncle. It's that light-bright motherfucker, Vaughn. Huh?"

She frowned. "Okay, now you're trippin'. It's not Vaughn."

She turned back toward the sink, hoping to end the conversation.

"Yeah, the fuck it is!" he snapped. "Ever since that block party, you been actin' different. You think you gonna leave me for that motherfucker?"

Before she could respond, he grabbed her arm, spinning her around to face him.

His grip was so tight she knew it would leave a mark.

"Please stop. You're hurting me," Psalm pleaded, struggling to pull away.

Jetson's face twisted in rage.

"Bitch," he spat—Before swinging the back of his hand across her face.

Psalm flew across the bathroom, hitting the floor, her body curling against the tub.

Pain radiated through her cheek.

Jetson knelt beside her and grabbed her face, forcing her to look at him.

"After everything I done for you, you ungrateful ass…"

He squeezed her jaw harder.

"You got another thing coming."

Psalm whimpered, her body trembling, her cheek stinging from the blow.

Jetson stared at her for a long moment, his chest rising and falling with heavy breaths. Then, his lips curled into a sneer.
"You gon' leave me for this nigga?"

His voice was low, dangerous.

He suddenly shoved her face to the side, a forceful mush that sent her head snapping back. "I'll kill your ass."
With that, he pushed himself up and stormed out of the bathroom, his footsteps heavy as he disappeared down the hall.

Psalm lay on the cold tile floor, gasping for air between sobs.

Her body shook violently as the weight of everything came crashing down. And for the first time, she felt truly trapped.
Tears streamed down her face as she curled into herself, crying hysterically, knowing deep down—

This wasn't over.

***

Vaughn and Blizz sped down the expressway, energy through the roof.

Omega had just hit them off with two bricks of that raw.

Dollar signs flooded their minds.

This was it.

They were about to start getting real paper.

Just yesterday, they were nothing but petty corner hustlers, scraping up what they could. But now?

They had the keys to the city.

Or at least, that's what they thought.

All they had to do was make that workflow, keep that re-up money right, and Omega would keep blessing them.

Vaughn glanced at Blizz and smirked.

Blizz grinned back, slapping his hand—their fiftieth dap of the night.

"We in the motherfuckin' game now, baby!" Vaughn said, excitement thick in his voice. "You motherfuckin' right we are," Blizz responded, his eyes gleaming.

They were ready to fuck the streets up.

But Vaughn knew they had to be smart about it.

***

"Listen, bro," Vaughn started, shifting into business mode. "If we gon' do this, we gotta do this shit right."

Blizz nodded, exhaling smoke from a fresh-rolled L.

"We ain't changin' up what we sell—soft and hard, straight raw. We got the best dope in the city right now. Uncut. Unstepped on. That shit is gonna sell itself."

Blizz nodded again, listening.

"When the money starts coming in, no flashy shit. No fuckin' up the money, Blizz."

Vaughn's tone turned serious as he stared Blizz down, already knowing his weakness.

Blizz loved to spend. He was a party animal. The type to blow stupid money in the club just to show out.

"No doubt," Blizz assured, but Vaughn wasn't convinced.

"We need a loyal crew," Vaughn continued, "niggas who can move the work and handle shit if it comes to that."

Blizz smirked at that part.

He knew exactly what Vaughn meant—niggas who wouldn't hesitate to lay the murder game down.

"We keep Omega paid, he keeps hittin' us off," Vaughn added.

"Most definitely," Blizz agreed.

Vaughn locked eyes with him.

"And last but not least—we don't let nothin' come between us. Not money, not cars, not hoes." Blizz nodded firmly, then they locked hands again.

"That's a fact, my nigga. Brothers till the end."

***

The red cherry Benz pulled up in front of Blizz's house. Vaughn put the car in park.

"Look, my nigga," Vaughn said, gripping the wheel, "I'ma hold the bricks at my crib till we figure out how we movin'. I'ma pull up first thing in the morning so we can get this shit together."

"That's a bet, my nigga. Get at me in the morning."

Blizz hopped out and shut the door, walking toward his house with confidence. Vaughn threw the car in drive.

"Alright, one."

***

A couple of minutes later, Vaughn pulled up, parked, and hopped out, bookbag in hand. It had been a long ass day.

As soon as he stepped inside, there he was—Roy, sitting on the couch in his drawers, TV dinner in one hand, a big-ass cup of red Kool-Aid in the other.

Roy's greasy ass lips smacked loudly as he turned his head toward Vaughn.

"What's up, youngin'? Everything good with you?" he asked, chewing with his mouth open. Vaughn ignored him.

He couldn't stand Roy.

Dude was a bum. He came and went as he pleased, never helping with shit, mooching off Dee Dee.

Vaughn knew the game.

Roy wasn't there for his mother.

He was there for a place to stay and to get high.

Vaughn walked past him straight to the kitchen, leaving Roy's hand hanging when he reached out for a dap.

***

Sitting at the kitchen table, slumped over, was Dee Dee—nodding off from her high. Vaughn just shook his head.

He went to the cabinet, grabbed a cup, and poured himself some juice.

The sight of his mother like this made him sick.

The anger bubbled inside him, boiling over as he slammed the fridge shut.

Dee Dee's head snapped up.

Drool was on her chin.

She wiped her mouth.

"Hey, Vaughn… you okay, son?" Her voice was weak.

Vaughn took a slow sip, refusing to turn around.

"I'm alright, Dee Dee."

That's all she was to him now. Dee Dee.

The day he caught her getting high was the day she stopped being Mom.

***

Just as he turned to leave, Roy was blocking the threshold.

"Hey, young blood," Roy said, leaning against the wall with his arms crossed. "Kitchen sink leakin', hallway light need fixin'."

Vaughn glared at him.

"Well, fix it then, nigga."

Roy chuckled, showing those yellow-ass teeth.

"Hell, this ain't my house."

Vaughn's patience snapped.

"That's a fact. So how 'bout you get your freeloadin' ass up outta here?" Roy stepped up, squaring his shoulders.

"Watch how you talk to me, youngin'."

Vaughn didn't budge.

"Or what?"

They stood chest to chest until Dee Dee's groggy voice broke the tension. "Y'all 'bout to blow my high… cut it out."

Vaughn shoved past Roy, bumping his shoulder as he walked away.

"We gon' finish this conversation later," Roy called after him.

No the fuck we won't, Vaughn thought, slamming his bedroom door.

***

Inside, he went straight to the closet, pulling out the two bricks.

He stared at them, feeling the weight of his future in his hands.

"This the beginning of something big."

He grabbed an empty sneaker box, tucked the bricks inside, and stacked it neatly with the rest. Just as he shut the closet, his door burst open.

"Vaughn!"

Little Jewel ran full speed, jumping into his arms.

Vaughn hugged her tight, swinging her around, his frustrations melting.

"I got my report card today!"

"Oh yeah? Let me see it."

Jewel proudly handed it over. Straight A's.

Vaughn smiled. "Proud of you, sis."

She grinned. "Not even one B!"

"And what do I always say?" Vaughn teased.

"You'll never catch me with a C or a D—'cause D's are for dummies!"

They laughed.

"That's right, baby girl. And what you gon' be when you grow up?"

"A doctor!" Jewel said proudly.

Vaughn nodded. "That's what's up, Dr. Jewel."

She gasped. "Oh! I need my doctor stuff!"

She sprinted out, returning with her fake hospital kit and a baby doll.

They played doctor and patient, Vaughn laughing as Jewel took her job way too seriously.

For the first time that day, Vaughn felt at peace.

At least with her, he could still believe in something good.

As Jewel's eyelids grew heavy, Vaughn chuckled.

"Come on, it's way past your bedtime. Plus, you got school in the morning."

She yawned, but didn't argue as Vaughn scooped her up into his arms and carried her to bed. Just as he turned to leave, her voice came, soft and tired.

"Vaughn?"

He paused. "What's up, princess?"

"Please don't ever leave me."

Her words hit him hard.

He swallowed. "I promise I'll never leave you, princess."

He smoothed her hair. "And if I ever do… I promise I'll always come back for you."

She sighed, barely above a whisper. "Okay."

As her breathing slowed, Vaughn just stood there, watching her. The one good thing left in his world.

Then, he cut off the lights and closed the door, leaving little Jewel sound asleep in the safety of her dreams.

Here's Chapter 8: No Witnesses, fully revised, immersive, and intense, with updated names and enhanced action, tension, and dialogue for even greater impact.

CHAPTER 7: NO WITNESSES

The work that Omega had given Blizz and Vaughn was flooding Hempstead, Long Island. In just a few days, they had taken over the entire city.

They had already re-upped twice, and now, Omega was dropping off ten bricks at a time.

A brick on the street went for $22,000, but Omega was letting them have it for $18,000—he was definitely showing love.

Vaughn and Blizz locked down nearly every corner store, paying the owners to let them hustle out front.

If the cops came through, they could duck inside and lock the door.

They played it smart, recruiting juveniles to move work—if the young hustlers got caught, they wouldn't face serious time, making them less likely to snitch.

***

Vaughn had a vision.

He wanted to package $10 vials of both cocaine and crack, attracting different clientele. To separate their product, he trademarked the dope with a signature stamp: Space Jam.

The vials had a sticker of Marvin the Martian on them.

Calling the demand crazy would be an understatement—if you weren't selling Space Jam, the fiends weren't even trying to shop.

But Vaughn knew they had to expand.

They had hustlers, but they needed muscle. That's when they decided to recruit Tec and Milli.

***

Tec and Milli were twin brothers from the hood.

Both tall and slim, long dreads past their shoulders.

These twins were the real deal—kill first, ask questions later. Their body count was so high, even they had lost track.

They were known as the Snitch Killers, and while the community feared them, they also respected them.

They were exactly who Blizz and Vaughn needed on the team. Vaughn had already reached out.

The twins accepted without hesitation.

Now, it was time to make it official.

***

Blizz and Vaughn pulled up on them in a big-body BMW X6—Blizz's new ride, paid for in straight cash.

Along with the car, he had copped a Cuban link and a bust-down Rolex, flaunting his success. Vaughn made a mental note to tell Blizz to keep a lower profile.

They'd have that conversation later.

Jumping out of the BMW X6, they dapped up the twins.

"Fellas, fellas, what's good with y'all?" Vaughn asked.

"Shit, everything is everything. The real question is, what's good with y'all niggas? Y'all been making a lot of noise around town, and me and my brother been itching to get next to y'all," Tec responded.

You could tell Tec and Milli apart because Milli always had a permanent mug and barely spoke. He was the silent assassin— just observing and nodding.

"Respect. Well, y'all definitely part of the team now, so let's get straight to business," Vaughn said.

"Me and Blizz got this whole side of town on lock. Since y'all know the area better than anyone, I'm putting y'all in charge. I'll hit y'all off with a few bricks later today—$19,500 a pop.**"

Vaughn studied their reaction.

Tec ran his fingers through his beard. "$19,500? Not a bad number at all." Milli nodded in agreement.

"Not at all. Especially when the dope is 100% pure, unstepped-on coke. You can cut it three, four times, and the fiends will still be going Kanye," Vaughn explained.

Tec smirked. "No doubt."

"Most importantly, me and Blizz are heading out to Wyandanch to take over. A few fools ain't gonna like the changes, so we need hitters who won't hesitate to get their hands dirty."

Tec smirked. "Oh, murder? That's our middle name, baby. We don't give a fuck about pushing a few niggas wigs back."

Milli rubbed his hands together, a devilish excitement gleaming in his eyes at the mention of killing.

***

Before Vaughn could respond, one of his little workers, Peanut, came running up, looking shook. "Yo, Vaughn, I was down the block serving, and these niggas told me I can't hustle there."

Vaughn's eyes narrowed. "What?"

"Yeah, some new Harlem niggas. They said it's their block. Told me if they catch anyone selling Space Jam, it's lit."

Blizz immediately patted his waist, making sure his Glock was on him. "Let's go see about these niggas."

Before he could take a step, Tec put a hand on his chest, stopping him. "Nah."

He turned to Peanut.

"Go back to that block and keep selling."

Peanut hesitated. "Huh?"

Tec's voice dropped an octave. "Don't make me repeat myself." Peanut nodded and went back.

The fiends were too thirsty for Space Jam, and Peanut caught two sales as soon as he touched back down.

That's when the three Harlem niggas, standing at a distance, started moving toward him. They had no idea this was their last time stepping foot on this street.

***

The trap had already been set.

Tec and Milli emerged from the alleyway, their movements quiet, calculated. Guns already raised.

Tec took the first shot—a clean, precise pop to the leader's head.

His skull cracked open before his body even hit the pavement.

Blood and brain matter sprayed onto the sidewalk, the impact so sudden that the second man froze in shock.

That hesitation cost him his life.

Before he could even reach for his piece, Milli stepped forward, arm steady, aim locked in. Four quick shots.

Two in the chest.

One in the neck.

One in the stomach.

His body folded like a chair, blood pooling beneath him as he gasped for air, his hands weakly pressing against the bullet wounds.

But Milli wasn't finished.

Standing over him, he tilted his head slightly, as if studying his agony. Then—BANG! BANG! BANG!

He put three more rounds into his face.

That was a closed casket for sure.

The third man turned to run.

Bad move.

Tec chased him down, hitting him twice in the back, the force sending him sprawling forward onto the pavement.

He scrambled, trying to crawl—his last effort to escape death. Tec wasn't about to let that happen.

He walked right up to him, stood over his trembling body, then pressed the barrel of his Glock against the back of his head.

A single shot ripped through his skull, splattering bone and flesh onto the curb. As quickly as the twins appeared, they were gone.
The twins were so nice they managed to leave the block, then came back wearing a new set of clothes and blended in with the crowd. Just to see if anyone had a case of loose lips while the police asked questions.

Nobody saw a thing.

Or at least, nobody who valued their life would speak on it. "Yeah them two niggas don't bullshit." Said Vaughn.

Vaughn and Blizz were about to slide out in the BMW X6 when a familiar face approached— Sada.

"Yo, what up?" Sada said, his tone calm but firm.

Blizz lifted his shirt slightly, showing off his Glock 40.

"You sure you wanna do this right here?" He nodded toward the police down the block.

Sada laughed, shaking his head.

"Relax, nigga. I ain't on that type of time."

He leaned in slightly, voice lowering.

"I came to tell y'all one thing—I want in."

That caught Vaughn and Blizz off guard.

"What you mean, you want in?" Vaughn asked, eyes narrowing.

Sada sucked his teeth. "What you mean, what do I mean? I want in on whatever y'all got going. It's obvious y'all eating."

Blizz frowned. "And why the fuck should we let you in?"

Sada smirked, his eyes cold and unreadable.

"Because I'm the reason y'all breathing fresh air."

Vaughn's face stayed emotionless, but his grip tightened on the wheel.

"I know y'all the motherfuckers who smoked Ronnie. And Vaughn—you know I know." The street felt silent for a moment. Tension thick enough to cut with a blade.

Sada kept talking, voice flat and serious.

"The D's picked me up the same night of the block party and started pressing me about who killed ol' boy," he said, his tone bitter.

"They beat my ass, burnt me with cigarette butts—did all types of grimy shit trying to make me squeal. Them low-down dirty bastards even planted coke on me, had me sitting in county for over thirty days."

Sada exhaled, shaking his head.

"I just got out yesterday."

Vaughn and Blizz exchanged looks.

They didn't need to say a word—they were reading each other's reactions. Was Sada telling the truth?

Was he really solid?

Or was he setting them up?

Sada noticed their hesitation and kept talking.

"Look, man, I ain't tryna blackmail y'all, and I damn sure ain't sayin' y'all owe me anything." His tone was steady, matter of fact.

"All I'm sayin' is—I held it down. I ain't fold, even under pressure. The least y'all can do is let a nigga get some money with y'all.

Simple as that."

He folded his arms.

"So what's it gonna be?"

Vaughn and Blizz didn't answer right away.

They were stuck.

If Sada was working with the police, bringing him in would be the beginning of the end. But if they shut him down, he could take what he knew straight to the cops—and that was a risk they couldn't afford.

Then there was a third option—maybe he was really loyal.

Maybe he could actually be an asset.

They were still in the process of building their team, and a solid soldier who could withstand police pressure was hard to come by.

After a brief pause, Vaughn spoke first.

His tone careful, unreadable.

"Look, we respect that you stood tall," he said.

"But me and my cuz gotta talk it over first. We'll get back to you." Sada stared at them both for a few seconds before nodding.

"Alright, bet. Y'all know where to find me."

Without another word, he turned and bopped down the street. Vaughn and Blizz watched him go.

The weight of that conversation sat heavy between them.

And just like that, they found themselves at a crossroads.

A single decision could determine whether they rose higher— Or fell harder.

And right now?

The streets were watching.

CHAPTER 8: FORBIDDEN DESIRES

Business Is Booming

Everything was going according to plan.

Space Jam was running through the streets, and the dollars kept rolling in. Vaughn and Blizz had made a calculated decision to bring Mugz onto the team. You know the saying—keep your friends close, but your enemies closer.

That was the philosophy they chose to live by.

To their surprise, Sada actually became an asset.

His bully tactics worked on the local dealers.

He gave them one choice—cop from him or become an enemy.

Nobody wanted to be on Sada's bad side, so the majority fell in line.

Every week, he was re-upping with Vaughn, copping at least two bricks. Despite their rocky history, Vaughn actually started to like Mugz.

The dude was solid.

He handled business.

He stayed loyal.

All the past tension didn't matter anymore.

**

Vaughn sat inside his SL-550 Benz, parked up, staring into the night.

He had everything—money, a fly foreign, designer clothes, women.

He couldn't complain.

But something still felt off.

Maybe that was the problem.

He had everything except that one thing every hustler needed—a real one.

Someone to hold him down.

Someone to ride through it all.

Someone to share his wins and losses.

Without that, everything else felt hollow.

And for the past few days, he couldn't stop thinking about Psalm.

The last time he saw her was at the block party.

School was out for the summer, and Vaughn made a mental note to find her. He needed to tell her how he really felt.

***

Before he could go deeper into his thoughts, his phone vibrated. A text from Astoria.

The neighborhood jump-off from Wyandanch.

Vaughn liked her, but he liked her head game even more.

She was a slim, light-skinned shorty with long, straight hair. What Vaughn didn't know?

She was madly in love with him.

The message read:

"I'm still upset with you for leaving me on the curb. You promised to take me on a dinner date and never showed."

Vaughn had completely forgotten about that. Too much had been going on that day.

He figured he should make it up to her.

He typed back:

"You're right, baby girl. I did, and I apologize. Let me make it up to you. Put on your best dress, get as cute as you can. Be ready at 9 PM—I'm taking you out."

He hit send.

Not even 30 seconds later, his phone buzzed again.

"Okay, daddy. LOL."

Vaughn sighed and tossed his phone into the cup holder.

Whoever said pimpin' was easy was a damn liar.

He put the car in drive and decided to make a few rounds to check on his blocks.

***

As Vaughn pulled onto his first stop, something caught his eye.

Psalm.

She was walking out of the corner store.

"Damn, that's crazy—I was just thinking about her."

Without hesitation, he pulled up beside her, lowered the passenger window, and called out. "Damn, lil' mama, what's your name?"

Psalm glanced over and half-smiled.

She couldn't help it—seeing Vaughn made her heart race.

Ever since the block party, she had thought about him a lot.

"Haha, very funny," she said, keeping it moving.

She didn't want to engage—if Jetson found out, he would kill her.

"Yo, jump in. Let me give you a ride home," Vaughn offered.

Psalm hesitated.

"Thanks, but I'm good. I don't wanna ride in your hot box," she replied. Vaughn chuckled.

"Girl, this ain't no stolen car. This my shit! I got the pink slip right here." He waved the paperwork, showing her the Benz was all cash.

She glanced but wasn't impressed.

"Come on, lil' mama. A ride home won't hurt."

Psalm stopped in her tracks.

"Just go where you're going. The last thing I need is someone seeing us and running back to Jetson."

Vaughn wasn't giving up.

"Alright, how 'bout this—I park, we smoke one, I roll up the windows so nobody sees you under the tint, then you go about your day."

He put his hands together, giving her puppy eyes. Psalm laughed.

"Okay. Just one blunt. Then I gotta go."

She got in.

***

Vaughn parked, pulled out his grabba leaf, and started rolling up.

Psalm sat back, watching him.

Everything about him was different now.

The Benz.

The clean interior.

The scent of Jimmy Choo cologne filling the air. His neatly done braids, his fresh lineup.

She found herself sneaking looks.

His demeanor had changed, too.

Everything about him screamed boss.

They talked.

One blunt turned into two.

Two turned into three.

Before she knew it, she was riding with him, feet on his dashboard, rolling while he collected money from his workers.

The conversation got deep.

Vaughn told her about growing up without a father, about his little sister, about his mother's addiction.

Psalm shared her past—being kicked out of her mom's house young, how she met Jetson, how she recently lost her uncle.

They lost track of time.

Before either of them realized, they were pulling up to the mall.

"What are we doing here? You gotta meet someone?" Psalm asked.

Vaughn smirked.

"Nah. I'm taking you shopping. And I ain't taking no for an answer." He stepped out, walked around, and opened her door.

Psalm hesitated.

But the way he carried himself, the way he spoke with authority—she didn't even protest.
She slid her arm through his, and they walked inside together.

At first, she felt nervous.

What if someone saw them?

But that feeling quickly faded.

For the first time in a long time, she felt happy.

***

By the time Vaughn dropped her home, she was dripping in designer. Psalm hesitated at the doorway.

"Vaughn, I really had a good time. Thank you for everything…"

Her head dropped slightly.

"But I don't know where we go from here."

Vaughn studied her for a second.

And in that moment, he knew—this wasn't the end.

It was just the beginning.

***

Psalm's head dropped.

She was torn.

She had Jetson breathing down her neck. But Vaughn made her feel alive.

"We need to be together," Vaughn said, placing his hand over his heart.

She stared into his intense gaze, then looked away.

She felt the same way.

But was it worth the risk?

"Just say the word, baby. I'll take you away from all this. You know I got you." She swallowed hard.

Everything was moving too fast.

"Let's just slow down," she said softly.

"If it's meant to be, it'll be… okay?"

She squeezed his hand gently.

Vaughn nodded, the heat in his eyes not fading.

"You got it, sweetheart."

He turned to leave.

"Wait, Vaughn."

He turned back.

Psalm grabbed both his hands, searching for words—but instead, she kissed him.

And just like that… everything changed.

She led him inside.

And when the door closed, there was no turning back.

***

As soon as the door shut behind them, they were all over each other.

Psalm's breath was ragged, her hands pulling him closer, her body pressing against his as she led him down the hall toward her bedroom.

Their tongues tangled, their breathing grew heavy, and his hands roamed her curves, gripping the fullness of her behind.

They stumbled into her bedroom, stripping their clothes in a rush.

Psalm stood before him, her almond skin glowing under the dim light.

Her long hair cascaded down her back, framing her toned waist and thick hips.

As she shed her shirt and bra, her perfectly round breasts bounced free, and when she slid out of her baggy pants, Vaughn took in the sight of her bare ass, firm and inviting.

Desire surged through him, straining against his designer jeans.

She stepped closer, her hand pressing against his hardness through the fabric, massaging him slow, deliberate strokes.

"I want it in my mouth," she whispered, her voice dripping with seduction as she unbuckled his belt and let his pants drop to the floor.

Vaughn's breath hitched as she freed him from his boxers, her fingers wrapping around his thick shaft.

She spit on him, coating him before taking him into her mouth, her eyes locked onto his.

Her tongue swirled around him, teasing, before she swallowed him deeper, her lips gliding along his girth.

His head tilted back, a deep groan escaping as he tangled his fingers in her hair, guiding her movements.

She stroked him in rhythm, her mouth working him over with skill until she pulled back, her lips glistening.

"I need you inside me," she breathed, her body trembling with need.

She turned, placing her hands on the bed, arching her back as she pushed her ass toward him, wiggling slightly in anticipation.

Vaughn stepped behind her, stroking himself, then pressed his tip against her dripping entrance. He grabbed a handful of her ass, spreading her open as he eased inside, inch by inch.

A sharp gasp left her lips as she adjusted to his size.

"Damn, you're so thick," she moaned, gripping the sheets.

He thrust slow at first, teasing her, then picked up the pace, his abdomen slapping against her ass with each stroke.

"Fuck me harder," she pleaded, her voice ragged with need.

Vaughn gripped her waist, pulling her back onto him with force, meeting each thrust with deep, relentless strokes.

The bed creaked beneath them, the room filled with the sound of skin against skin.

A picture frame of her and Jetson fell from the wall, crashing to the floor, but neither of them noticed.

"You like this dick?" he growled, smacking her ass.

"Yes, Daddy," she moaned, pushing back against him.

He drove into her deeper, her walls tightening around him.

Sweat dripped down his back as he pounded into her, his grip firm on her hips.

"Are you mine now?" he demanded.

"Yes, baby, I'm all yours," she whimpered.

Her body trembled as she neared the edge, her moans turning to cries of pleasure. "Don't pull out," she begged, her voice barely a whisper.

That was all it took.

Vaughn lost control, his body tensing as he buried himself deep, releasing inside her.

A shudder rolled through him, and he collapsed onto the bed, spent.

Psalm crawled up beside him, resting her head on his chest as they caught their breath. For a while, they just lay there, tangled in the sheets, lost in their thoughts.

The sex had been incredible, but beneath the satisfaction, something lingered—something unspoken.

***

Vaughn's moment of peace was interrupted by the vibration of his phone. He reached over, pulling it from his pocket.

The screen lit up with a message from Astoria.

"Fuck you, motherfucker."

His eyes flicked to the time—11:47 PM. Damn. He had forgotten again.

With a sigh, he tossed the phone onto the nightstand and pulled Psalm closer, unaware that Astoria was about to become a problem he wasn't ready for.

CHAPTER 9: THE MONSTER AWAKENS

Vaughn sat at the head of the round table, his eyes scanning each person seated before him. Around him sat Blizz, Sada, Tec, Milli, and Psalm.

This was his team—the family he had chosen.

And now, it was time for the takeover.

"If you're sitting at this table, I want you to know something—you're my family," Vaughn began, his voice firm, unwavering.

The room fell silent.

"Look to your left. Now to your right."

They did.

"That person sitting next to you? They'll take a bullet for you. Because that's what family does." Vaughn stood up, pacing the room, his presence commanding.

"This team is built on loyalty and honor. Respect each other. Keep each other's best interests at heart—because if we don't have that, we have nothing."

He paused, letting his words settle.

"Watch each other's backs. You do that, and we'll win. No doubt about it."

Reaching down, he grabbed a duffel bag and dumped its contents onto the table.

Stacks of neatly wrapped bricks tumbled out.

The weight of the moment pressed down on everyone at the table.

"Right here? That's fifty bricks of straight raw," Vaughn declared. "I'm about to take over this whole motherfucking city.

We're about to get rich.

But if we're not on the same page, everything we build will come crashing down like a ton of real bricks."

He grabbed a champagne glass, raising it in the air.

"To family."

Everyone lifted their glasses.

"To family," they echoed, clinking glasses before downing their drinks.

Vaughn set his empty glass down and turned to Blizz.

"Blizz, I need you to take ten bricks to your people in Jamaica, Queens.

They can either buy or take them on consignment. If they refuse, let them know bullets will rain on their block before the sun comes up."

Blizz nodded in understanding. "Tec, Milli," Vaughn continued.

"Take ten and hit Suffolk County. Let them niggas know— it's either get down or lay down. I want Space Jam on every block. Go as far as Riverhead if you need to."

He then turned to Sada.

"You're rolling with me to One Dance tomorrow. Same rules apply." Everyone nodded, locked in.

Blizz smirked. "And what about her?" he asked, nodding toward Psalm. Before Vaughn could answer, Psalm stood and walked over to him.

She draped an arm around his neck and pressed a kiss to his lips before turning to the group.

"My job is to be my man's eyes and ears—to watch his back and make sure the money stays right," she said confidently.

Vaughn grinned.

"Damn right," he said, looking down at her with approval.

"Alright, niggas," Vaughn said, handing out the bricks.

"Let's get to work."

***

Roy slumped on the loveseat, the TV playing in the background.

The crack pipe dangled from his lips as he nodded in and out of his high.

82

The Fresh Prince of Bel-Air flickered on the screen, but his glazed eyes barely registered the movement.

The front door creaked open, startling him.

Dee Dee and Little Jewel stepped inside, struggling with heavy laundry bags.

"Hey, baby," Dee Dee said, setting her bags down and walking over to plant a kiss on his cheek. "Took us forever at the laundromat, but we got it done."

Roy mumbled, flipping through the channels with half-lidded eyes.

Jewel turned to head back outside for the last bag, but before she could step out, Roy's rough hand snatched her wrist.

"Hey, Sunshine," he slurred, gripping her tightly.

"How's my baby doing?"

Jewel winced.

"Ouch! Let go! You're hurting me!" she cried, yanking her arm away before darting out the door. Something about Roy always made Jewel uneasy.

She stayed out of his way as much as possible.

Dee Dee returned from the kitchen and flopped onto Roy's lap.

"You got some left in that pipe for me?" she asked, her eyes hungry for another hit. Roy smirked, pulling a dime rock from his pocket and twirling it between his fingers. Dee Dee's mouth watered.

She reached for it, but he pulled away, teasing her.

"Come on, Roy. Stop playing with me," she whined, her eyes fixed on the rock. Roy chuckled darkly.

"What you gonna do for me?"

He lit the pipe, inhaled deeply, and then blew a cloud of smoke into her face.

"Whatever you want, baby," she pleaded. Roy wasn't interested in her this time.

He glanced toward Jewel's room.

"I want her."

Dee Dee's blood ran cold.

"Don't do that, baby," she said quickly, pressing her body against him. "I'm all the woman you need."

But Roy wasn't interested.

"No," he said, voice cold.

"I want her."

Dee Dee froze.

"She's ten," she whispered, desperation creeping into her voice. Roy sighed, shaking his head.

"Bitch, get off me," he snapped, shoving her to the floor.

Dee Dee gasped, staring up at Roy in horror as he grabbed his jacket and made his way toward the front door to leave.

She knew what he was about to do.

But the crack had her too weak to stop him.

"Baby, wait," she whimpered.

Roy paused at the door, smirking

He had her right where he wanted her.

"Give me the pipe," she whispered, sealing her deal with the devil.

Roy dropped the pipe beside her and strode toward Jewel's door.

He pushed it open.

***

Jewel sat on the edge of her bed, watching TV.

The moment she saw Roy, she tensed.

"Hey, baby doll," he cooed, shutting the door behind him.

Jewel's stomach churned.

She knew she was in trouble.

"Mommy!" she tried to scream, but Roy cut her off.

"Mommy had to run to the store," he lied, his voice low, dangerous. "No need to scream. We're just gonna play a little game."

Tears welled in Jewel's eyes.

Roy sat beside her, his rough hand sliding through her hair—then down her back—then lower—his crusty hands made their way between her Virgin thighs, parting her legs open.

A car door slammed outside.

Then came voices—one familiar, one female.

Roy froze.

Vaughn.

His hand shot over Jewel's mouth.

"You better not tell anyone," he hissed into her ear.

"Or I'll be back to finish what I started."

He jumped up, fastened his pants, and rushed out of the room. Dee Dee was still slumped on the floor, lost in her high.

***

The front door swung open.

Vaughn and Psalm stepped inside, a duffel bag in hand.

Vaughn took one look at Roy, then at Dee Dee, and shook his head.

"Nigga, let me hold something," Roy grinned, rubbing his hands together. Vaughn scoffed.

"Yeah, whatever."

Handing the duffel to Psalm, he turned down the hall.

"Go count this up, baby. It's a lot. We gonna be up all night."

Psalm disappeared into the bedroom while Vaughn knocked on Jewel's door. "Princess, you okay?"

Jewel, still trembling, stayed under the covers.

But hearing Vaughn's voice soothed her. "Yes," she whispered.

Vaughn frowned.

"You been crying?"

She forced a smile.

"No, I just woke up."

Vaughn exhaled slowly.

"Alright," he said, kissing her forehead.

"Get some rest, Doodle Butt."

He left the room, unaware of the horror he had just prevented. But that wouldn't last long.

Back in his room, Vaughn found Psalm counting stacks of bills.

It took them all night—seven hours, to be exact.

By the time they finished, the clock read 2 AM.

Over a million dollars counted, brick by brick.

Blizz and Psalm both flopped onto the bed, exhausted.

"I'm really glad you moved in, baby," Vaughn said with a smirk.

"Would've taken me all day to count that shit by myself."

Psalm playfully punched his arm.

"Let me find out that's the only reason you wanted me here."

Vaughn chuckled, lighting a Fresh Rolled blunt, taking a deep pull before passing it to her.

"Nah, baby, you know I couldn't have you staying with that bitch-ass nigga," he said, referring to Jetson.

Psalm laughed, inhaling before handing the blunt back.

"I still can't believe you answered my phone when he called." Vaughn exhaled a slow cloud of smoke.

"Fuck that nigga," he said, dismissively.

"I'm about to grab something to drink. You want anything?"

Psalm shook her head as he handed her back the blunt.

Vaughn made his way to the kitchen.

In the living room, Roy was slumped on the loveseat, dead asleep. Dee Dee lay sprawled across the couch, knocked out.

Vaughn poured himself a glass of Kool-Aid and was about to head back when a muffled sound caught his ear.

Crying.

His eyes narrowed.

His heart thumped harder with each step.

He pushed open Jewel's door.

She lay curled up beneath her covers, sobbing.

Vaughn sat beside her, voice soft but firm.

"Doodle Butt, what's wrong?"

She didn't answer at first, just buried her face deeper into the sheets.

"Come on, baby girl, talk to me," he pressed.

She sniffled, then whispered,

"Nothing. I'm just cold."

Vaughn frowned.

"Baby, the heat's on ninety-five. I know that's not it. Tell me what's really wrong."

Jewel trembled.

Then, her resolve broke, and she burst into harder sobs. Vaughn wrapped his arms around her, holding her tight. "Come on, princess, tell me so I can fix it," he murmured. She gasped between sobs, struggling to breathe.

Then, she finally broke.

"It's Roy," she choked out.

Vaughn's entire body stiffened.

His muscles tensed.

His grip on her shoulders tightened slightly.

"What about Roy?" he asked, his voice now deadly calm.

Jewel covered her face, ashamed.

Vaughn gently pulled her hands away.

"Baby, did he touch you?"

Tears streamed down her face as she nodded.

Vaughn felt his stomach drop.

His fists clenched.

His heartbeat roared in his ears.

"Where?" he asked, his voice low and dangerous.

She pointed to her backside.

Vaughn shot to his feet.

His vision blurred with rage.

Jewel jumped out of bed, clinging to him, holding onto his waist.

"Please, Vaughn! Don't say anything," she begged, her small hands gripping his shirt. "He said if I told anyone, he'd come back and finish what he started."

A silent storm built inside Vaughn.

His breathing was heavy, erratic.

His pulse pounded.

His blood boiled.

He crouched down to her level, placing his hands gently on her shoulders.

"Listen to me, princess," he said, his voice calmer now, but no less deadly.

"That will never happen again.

You did the right thing by telling me."

Jewel wiped her eyes, still shaking.

"Now, I need you to go into your closet," he instructed.

"Don't come out until I tell you. Okay?"

She nodded and ran inside, shutting the door behind her.

Vaughn turned and stormed out.

Roy was about to die.

Vaughn stormed into his room, his face hard as stone.

Psalm sat up immediately, sensing the shift in his energy.

"Baby, what's wrong?" she asked, voice laced with concern.

He didn't answer.

She watched as he grabbed his Glock 19 9mm from the dresser, checked the clip, then chambered a round.

Psalm's breath caught in her throat.

She knew—something serious was about to go down.

***

Vaughn walked straight into the living room.

Roy was still slumped in the chair, dead asleep.

The TV flickered, the glow reflecting off his greasy skin. Without hesitation, Vaughn raised the gun—and smashed the butt of it across Roy's face.

A sickening crunch echoed through the room.

Roy jerked awake, a blood-curdling yell escaping his lips.

He grabbed his forehead, blood pouring between his fingers.

"Oh shit! Man—Damn! What the fuck?!" he groaned, disoriented.

Vaughn didn't say a word.

He grabbed Roy by the collar and jammed the barrel of the Glock against his skull.

"You sick, perverted motherfucker," Vaughn growled through clenched teeth.

Roy's eyes bulged in panic.

"H-Huh? What you talking about, man?" he stammered, hands raised in surrender. His voice trembled—he knew.

He knew he was about to die.

***

Behind them, Dee Dee stirred awake.

She rubbed her eyes, still groggy from her high. "Vaughn, what on earth are you doing?" she mumbled. Vaughn snapped his gaze toward her.

"This creep-ass boyfriend of yours has been touching on Jewel," he spat. Dee Dee's face fell.

She didn't even deny it.

She just lowered her head in shame.

Vaughn studied her expression.

A slow realization dawned on him.

"You knew," he whispered, disbelief laced in his voice.

Dee Dee didn't respond.

She just sat there, silent.

Vaughn's fists clenched.

"You fucking knew," he repeated, shaking his head in disgust.

Roy tried to plead.

"Hold on, brother! I ain't molest nobody, you trippin'!" he begged. His heart hammered in his chest.

He saw it in Vaughn's eyes—there was no way out of this.

Vaughn's grip tightened on the gun.

"You wanna touch my sister?" he snarled—then brought the butt of the Glock down on Roy's skull—again.

***

Roy yelped in agony.

His teeth cracked, his head snapped to the side, blood dripping from his nose, his mouth, his busted lips.

But Vaughn saw nothing but red.

He smashed the gun across Roy's face again. And again. And again.

Roy's body slumped, barely conscious, his face an unrecognizable mess of blood and bruises. "Vaughn, stop!" Dee Dee shrieked— but she didn't dare step in.

She knew this was long overdue.

Vaughn wasn't done.

He grabbed Roy by the hair, yanked his head back, and pressed the gun to his lips. Roy whimpered, his lips quivering in terror.
"Open your mouth, you sick motherfucker," Vaughn ordered.

Roy was barely responsive, but his lips parted in weak surrender.

Vaughn shoved the barrel inside his mouth.

And pulled the trigger.

The shot ripped through the house, shaking the walls.

The back of Roy's head exploded, blood and brain matter splattering the wall behind him. His lifeless body slumped in the chair, his blood pooling beneath him.

Dee Dee gasped, hand over her mouth, before doubling over and vomiting onto the floor. Psalm stood frozen, hands covering her mouth, eyes wide with shock.

Vaughn turned to her, breathing heavily, his chest rising and falling rapidly.

"Call the twins. Tell them to come clean this up," he instructed, his voice cold, emotionless. Psalm nodded, still shaken, before reaching for her phone.

Vaughn turned back to Dee Dee, who sat sobbing on the floor.

"I'm moving out."

His voice was sharp, final.

"And I'm taking Jewel with me."

Dee Dee didn't argue.

She just rocked back and forth, mumbling to herself, her body shaking. Vaughn glanced at Roy's lifeless body one last time.

His first murder.

But it damn sure wouldn't be his last.

CHAPTER 10: TRUTH & CONTROL

Vaughn still couldn't believe it.

His mother had known—she had known Roy was molesting Jewel, and she hadn't done a damn thing to stop it. Not only that, but when he confronted her, she hadn't even tried to deny it.

And if he ever found out she had sold her daughter's innocence for crack? That she had let it happen willingly?

He wouldn't be able to stop himself from killing her too. That's why he packed up their shit and left.

Now, he had a new spot in Coram, Long Island—away from the filth, away from the poison. He was knee-deep in the game, and until he made it to the highest level and walked away, he had one mission: protect his family at all costs.

And that included Psalm.

Vaughn glanced over at her from the driver's seat. His mind was clouded with dark thoughts, but when he looked at her, something inside him softened.

He was falling for her. Hard.

He had never felt this way before. Something about Psalm made him want to be better. Maybe it was love—real love. He was used to having different chicks whenever he wanted, but for the first time, he didn't need anyone else.

She was the one.

And Psalm? She was just as deep in it as he was.

She had fallen for Vaughn since the very first night they were together. It was more than lust—he made her feel wanted, safe. Unlike Jetson, who had treated her like a possession, Vaughn made her feel free.

He didn't judge her. He didn't control her. He just loved her for who she was.

For the first time in her life, she had found someone she could truly call family.

She sat in the passenger seat, sneaking glances at him, her heart warm with a kind of affection she never thought she'd have. He made her feel like a queen—like she was untouchable.

But then, something caught her attention.

A black Suburban.

It had been following them for the last ten minutes. Her stomach tightened.

"Baby," she said, voice low but urgent. "That black truck has been behind us since we got off the expressway."

Vaughn turned the music down, his eyes shifting to the rearview mirror. His jaw clenched.
Fuck.

The Suburban was three cars behind them.

He made a right turn off the main street. The Suburban did the same. He took three more right turns, circling the block.

The truck followed. Every single time.

"Yeah, they're on us," he confirmed.

He reached into the console, grabbed a bag of weed, and handed it to Psalm. "Put this in your pussy," he ordered.

She didn't hesitate. She stuffed the bag into her panties just as red and blue lights flashed from the Suburban's front grille.

D's.

Cops.

Vaughn hit a hidden button near his radio. The stereo screen flipped down, revealing a secret compartment.

With quick precision, he pulled out the empty tray, placed his pistol inside, and slid it back in. Another press of the button, and the radio flipped back up, sealing the weapon away.

Then, he pulled the Benz over.

His hands went straight to the steering wheel.

This was New York. Cops were dirty as fuck, and one wrong move? They'd put him down on sight.

He rolled his window down and waited.

A tall, grimy-looking white man with slicked-back hair approached—Detective Grayson. He took one last drag from his cigarette, flicked it onto the pavement, and blew a cloud of smoke into Vaughn's face.

"Get out the car," he said in a raspy voice, removing his sunglasses. Vaughn didn't flinch.

"If you don't have probable cause, I'm not getting out of shit," Vaughn shot back, knowing his rights.

But he didn't know Detective Grayson.

The cop pulled his gun from his holster and pressed it against Vaughn's temple.

"Now, get your ass out this car before I your brains out all over that pretty bitch of yours."

On the passenger side, Detective Vega had Psalm in her sights, her hand resting on her holster. Psalm's heart pounded. She turned to Vaughn.

"Baby, just get out," she whispered.

Vaughn clenched his jaw, then opened the door.

Grayson patted him down and led him to the back of the car.

Vega pulled Psalm out next and began searching the vehicle.

Vaughn folded his arms, leaning against the hood.

"Sorry I had to get a little hostile with you back there," Grayson said, lighting another cigarette. "But that seems to be the only way you youngins understand."

Vaughn stared at him, rage boiling beneath his skin.

Grayson exhaled smoke.

"You familiar with the name Elroy Stevens?"

Vaughn didn't blink.

"Maybe I am, maybe I ain't," he said coolly. "Why?"

Grayson took another drag.

"I'll tell you why," he said. "His body was found floating in the fucking Hudson River." Vaughn stayed silent.

"Autopsy showed his face was smashed in, bones broken, and his brains scattered like confetti. When we ID'd him, turns out your mother's address was his last known residence."

Vaughn didn't flinch.

"So what?"

Grayson's nostrils flared.

"I'll tell you what," he said, stepping closer. "My theory? He was fucking your ole lady, and your bitch-ass couldn't stand it—so you killed him and moved out."

Vaughn's temper exploded.

He lunged forward, but Grayson's hand shot to his gun. "Go ahead," Grayson taunted. "Try me, boy."

Psalm stepped between them.

"Enough!" she snapped. "We're done answering questions. If you wanna talk, here's our lawyer's number."

Just then, Detective Vega walked back around.

"It's clean," she said.

She turned to Psalm, narrowing her eyes.

"You look familiar. Have we met?"

Psalm hesitated, then cleared her throat.

"Yeah," she said. "You both are supposed to be working the case of my uncle's murder." "My uncle, Ronnie Johnson."

Vaughn's heart dropped.

His stomach twisted.

He had helped kill her uncle.

How the fuck did he not know?

Detective Grayson glanced at Vaughn, noticing the slight shift in his body language.

But Vaughn masked it.

Grayson smirked.

"You're free to go," he said.

As Vaughn opened his car door, Grayson called out— "Hey, Vaughn... Tell your boy Blizz I like the new Scat Pack Challenger he bought yesterday. Nice ride."

Vaughn sped off.

His mind spun.

The D's were on his ass.

They were trying to crack Roy's murder. Trying to solve Ronnie's case.

And now? His girl was the niece of the man he helped kill. How the fuck was he gonna tell her?

***

Vaughn's mind was spinning.

He had to tell Psalm about Ronnie.

If he kept it a secret and she found out on her own, she'd feel betrayed. Worse, she'd feel like she had been sleeping with the enemy.

And then he'd lose her for sure.

But if he came clean now, maybe she'd understand.

This happened before they got together. He had no idea Ronnie was her uncle at the time. Yeah... maybe she'd understand.

Vaughn pulled into a gas station and parked at the pump, gripping the steering wheel tight. Just spit it out, Vaughn.

"Baby, I gotta tell you something," he started.

But before he could say another word, Psalm cut him off.

"Okay, let me just run inside and pay for the gas real quick," she said. "You want anything?" "Nah, I'm good," Vaughn replied, swallowing his nerves.

Psalm hopped out and walked toward the store.

Vaughn exhaled sharply, frustrated. Fuck. He couldn't even get the words out.

He shook his head. Wait till I tell Blizz this shit.

He sat in silence, waiting.

But then—something caught his eye.

Psalm had stepped out of the store.

But she wasn't alone.

Standing in front of her was Jetson.

Vaughn's blood boiled instantly.

His hand shot to the secret compartment. Button pressed. Glock 40 in hand.

He was out the car in seconds.

Before Jetson could react, Vaughn was on him—gripping his throat, slamming him against the gas station's front door.

The barrel of the Glock pressed hard into Jetson's stomach.

"Look, you bitch-ass nigga," Vaughn snarled. "This ain't your shorty no more. She belongs to me now, aight? If I ever catch you talking to her again, my gun gonna go off. We clear?"

Jetson's face drained of color. He looked like he was about to piss himself. "Y-yeah, man, we clear," he stammered.

Vaughn turned to Psalm.

"Get in the car. We out."

She obeyed without a word, slipping into the passenger seat.

Vaughn slid behind the wheel, his jaw clenched tight.

The silence in the car was thick.

Then—"The fuck was you doing talking to that nigga?" Vaughn asked, his tone sharp.

Psalm hesitated. "I wasn't, baby. He started talking to me first. I was telling him it was over for good."

Vaughn wasn't trying to hear it.

"Yeah, well, I better not ever catch you talking to that nigga again," he snapped. Psalm lowered her head. "Okay," she whispered.

But Vaughn wasn't done.

"Matter of fact—get out."

Psalm's head snapped up.

"What?"

"You heard me. Get out my car." She stared at him in disbelief.

Then, anger flashed across her face. She grabbed her purse, swung the door open, and stepped out.

She slammed the door behind her.

Vaughn mashed the gas, peeling off, leaving Psalm standing at the pump. But he wasn't really leaving her.

He drove about a quarter-mile up the block, then made a U-turn.

Less than three minutes later, he was back at the gas station.

Psalm was still standing by the pump.

And Jetson?

Still there too.

Vaughn pulled up, hopped out, and walked straight toward Psalm.

"Did this nigga say anything to you while I was gone?" he asked.

Psalm shook her head. "No."

Vaughn smirked, turning his attention to Jetson.

"See, I just wanted to show you what type of nigga he is," Vaughn said. He motioned toward Jetson.

"This nigga a bitch. He wouldn't even check on you. He wouldn't even make sure you was good."

He turned back to Psalm.

"He wouldn't protect you if some shit popped off. Like I said, don't talk to this bitch-ass nigga again."

Then he motioned toward the car. "Come on. Let's go."

Psalm climbed back into the passenger seat, silent.

Vaughn followed, slid behind the wheel, and peeled off.

Jetson stood frozen at the pump, feeling like the weak-ass nigga he was.

CHAPTER 11: THE SETUP

Music blasted from the stereo, vibrating through the smoke-filled living room.

Astoria swayed on top of the coffee table, hips rolling to the beat, putting on a show for the three men lounging on the couch. They were locked in, blunt smoke curling around them, already knowing what was about to happen.

Astoria was the neighborhood jump-off, and tonight, she was theirs. She lifted her shirt, revealing a perfect set of D-cup breasts.
"Yeah, take that shit off, baby," one of them urged.

Astoria moaned softly, squeezing her own breasts, the Hennessy in her system making her bold.

"Come down here and let us tap that ass," another man called out, his jeans tightening as he watched her.

"Okay, Daddy," she purred, "just give me another shot first."

One of them stood, bottle in hand, and poured liquor down her throat, some of it spilling onto her chest. They all laughed— Astoria included.

Sliding off the table, she stood in front of them, pulling her pants down to her ankles. Her light-skinned, plump ass bounced as she hopped, making their jaws drop.

"Smack it," she teased, glancing over her shoulder.

Smack!

One of them obeyed, leaving a red handprint on her cheek. Astoria giggled. "Y'all ready to get this party started?" she asked. "Hell yeah," they said in unison.

They were rock hard and ready to run a train on her.

"Let me hit the bathroom real quick," she said, pulling her pants back up. "Hurry up!" one of them yelled.

As she disappeared down the hallway, the three men sparked another blunt and passed it around.

"Ayo, tell me why some Hempstead niggas pulled up on me yesterday?" one of them said, exhaling smoke. "Talking about they heard we runnin' the town and we gotta cop work from them now. Sayin' if we don't, we ain't gonna like what's coming."

"And what you tell them?" one of his homies asked.

"I told them niggas to suck my dick. We ain't copping from nobody. If they want war, then bring it." He pulled his pistol from his waistband, his ego swelling. "Fuck wrong with them niggas?"

The others nodded in agreement, not feeling the idea of anyone trying to take their position.

"Ayo, Red," the leader said, turning to his boy, "go check on my son upstairs. We got this music blasting mad loud and shit."

"Aight," Red replied, heading up the stairs.

***

Astoria was in the bathroom, phone in hand. She typed a quick message to Vaughn. I unlocked the front door. Come now.

Outside, Vaughn, Blizz, and Sada sat in the car, waiting.

Vaughn's phone buzzed. He checked the screen, then looked at his crew.

"It's showtime, fellas. Let's go."

The three stepped out of the car, guns in hand, moving in silence toward the house. Just as Astoria said, the door was unlocked. They slipped inside.

Two of the men were still sitting on the couch, backs to the door, oblivious.

Sada struck first, slamming the butt of his gun into one of their heads. The man hit the floor with a thud.

"Get the fuck down!" Blizz and Vaughn barked.

The second man froze, then slowly laid on his belly, confusion and fear written all over his face. Fuck. This bitch set us up.

Sada and Blizz patted them down, stripping them of their pistols. Vaughn squatted beside the leader, staring him dead in the eyes.

"You was talking all that shit," Vaughn said, shaking his head. "Didn't I tell you that you wasn't gonna like what was coming?"

The leader said nothing, just lay there, his face twisted with regret.

"Look, man, it ain't too late," he finally stammered. "We can still do business. We'll cop dope from y'all, I swear."

"Oh, now you wanna do business?" Vaughn laughed, shaking his head. "I don't know, might be too late for that."

"Y'all bitch-ass niggas, get up. Sit on the couch," Blizz ordered. The men obeyed, fear written all over them.

"I'ma say this one time and one time only," Blizz said, cocking his gun. "One of y'all take me to the safe. Act stupid, and I'll empty the whole clip on you."

The one Sada knocked out earlier groggily stood and led Blizz to the back room. The leader sat stiff, sweat dripping down his temple.

"Come on, man," he pleaded. "Y'all can take the money and bricks. Just don't kill me. I got a son upstairs."

Sada and Vaughn kept their guns trained on him.

"Chill," Vaughn said. "If everything checks out with the safe, we might let you live." Then—a single gunshot rang out from the back.

Silence.

Blizz emerged moments later, two duffel bags in hand, blood specks on his shirt. "Everything's everything?" Vaughn asked.

Blizz nodded.

The leader's breath came fast. He raised his hands in surrender.

"Hold up! I thought you said if everything was good, y'all would let me live!"

Vaughn smirked.

"I said we might."

A second later, gunfire erupted.

Vaughn and Sada emptied their clips, leaving the leader slumped on the couch, his body riddled with holes.

***

Upstairs, Red had seen it all.

His heart pounded as he locked the bedroom door.

The little boy ran over, gripping Red's leg.

"Uncle Red, I'm scared! Please take me with you!"

Red looked down, tears stinging his eyes.

"I gotta go, little man," he whispered, shoving the boy aside.

He climbed out the second-story window and dropped into the front yard. Fuck that. He had to get out.

Red sprinted to his car, peeling out of the driveway, hands shaking on the wheel. He sped through the streets, running stop signs, trying to put as much distance as possible between himself and that house.

But at the next intersection—BAM!

A car slammed into his driver's side, flipping him into the passenger seat. Dazed, Red coughed through the smoke filling his car.

His vision blurred, but when he looked up, his stomach sank.

The passenger door of the other car opened.

Milli stepped out, AK-47 in hand.

Red's instincts kicked in. He ducked—

Too late.

Milli fingered the trigger, unloading 50 shots into the car.

The bullets tore through metal, glass, and flesh.

When the clip was empty, Red was nothing but a bloodied corpse in the front seat. Milli climbed back into the car, and Tec sped off.

***

The Stash House

Vaughn and his crew sat around the dining table, stacks of cash and bricks spread out in front of them.

"Fourteen bricks, seven hundred thousand, and still counting," Sada said, licking his thumb as he flipped through another band of bills.

They had just pulled a million-dollar lick.

"Damn, them suckas was getting money," Tec laughed. "Too bad they can't enjoy it." He leaned back, rolling a blunt, eyes flicking to Vaughn.

"Yo, you need to tell the plug to double us up on the next shipment. Me and my brother can handle at least fifty of them things. If you scared to tell him, take me with you next time. I'll tell him myself."

Vaughn's jaw tightened.

This was the third time Tec had brought up the plug. He didn't like it.
Vaughn locked eyes with him.

"Let me tell you something, nigga," he said, voice cold. "For one, I ain't scared of nobody. And two—I'll tell the plug whatever the fuck I want, whenever the fuck I want."

Tec leaned back, smirking, but Vaughn wasn't laughing. Something about Tec wasn't sitting right with him.

Vaughn waved Tec off and nodded toward Blizz. "Let me holla at you outside."

Blizz followed him out, shutting the door behind them. He reached into his pocket, popped a perk, and tossed it back, washing it down with a quick swig of water.

"What's up, brother?" he asked, wiping his mouth.

Vaughn exhaled sharply, tension tightening his jaw. He ran a hand over his head before locking eyes with Blizz.

"Yo, we hot."

Blizz frowned, leaning against the porch railing.

"What you mean?"

Vaughn shook his head, pacing slightly. His mind had been racing ever since the stop.

"I was riding with Psalm earlier, and these two dirty-ass detectives pulled me over. Started asking questions about Roy, talking like they think I killed him and shit." He paused, watching Blizz's reaction. "Then one of them mentioned you."

Blizz perked up, intrigued now.

"Said he like that new Scat Pack you got," Vaughn continued, his tone low and serious. "Nigga said he watching us. I told you—stop being so fuckin' flashy. You bringing unnecessary attention."

Blizz pulled out his phone, scrolling through Instagram, barely fazed.

"Man, fuck them cops. Them niggas don't know shit. If they did, we'd be locked up already. Don't trip, bro."

Vaughn stopped pacing, his eyes darkening.

He couldn't believe how casually Blizz was taking this.

"Nah, nigga. I do need to trip because they on to us," Vaughn snapped, his voice rising. "You gotta start moving smarter before you get all of us locked the fuck up."

Blizz finally looked up, seeing the fire in Vaughn's eyes. He sighed, nodding just to defuse the tension.

"Aight, bro. I'll move a little smarter."

Vaughn studied him, trying to gauge if he really meant it. He wasn't sure.

"And that's not even the last of it."

Blizz tensed slightly. "What now?"

Vaughn hesitated, the weight of what he was about to say pressing down on him. His chest tightened, but he had to get it out.

"Remember that nigga Ronnie? The one Omega sent us to hit?"

Blizz smirked, memories of the job flashing through his mind.

"How could I forget?"

"Well, tell me why the same detectives working Roy's case are on Ronnie's, too?" Vaughn rubbed his temples.

"And it turns out that nigga Ronnie? He's Psalm's uncle." Blizz's face twisted in disbelief.

He let out a low whistle, shaking his head.

"The fuck? Damn… small-ass world."

Vaughn nodded grimly, the weight of the situation crushing him.

He had replayed it over and over in his head—Psalm's smile, her laugh, the way she trusted him with everything.

But she had no clue the man she was falling for had a hand in taking her uncle's life. Blizz eyed him closely.

"So what you gonna do? You gonna tell her?"

Vaughn exhaled, looking away. His chest felt tight.

"I was gonna, man. But I didn't get the chance."

He shook his head.

"That shit gonna crush her."

Blizz scoffed, stepping closer.

"That's why you don't tell her, nigga." His voice was firm now.

"We takin' this shit to the grave."

He studied Vaughn, making sure his words hit.

"Plus, what if you do tell her, and this bitch gets you locked up for life?"

Vaughn's stomach twisted.

He wanted to believe Psalm was different—that she wouldn't betray him.

But how could he be sure?

"Nah, man. She ain't like that," he muttered, but it felt weaker this time, less certain. Blizz smirked, catching it.
"Whatever you say, bro." Then, switching gears, he grinned.

"But what's up, nigga? I got a section at Soho House tonight—twenty bad bitches say they pulling up. You rolling?"

Vaughn shook his head.

"Not tonight. Me and Psalm got a movie date in about forty-five minutes." Blizz narrowed his eyes.
"A movie date?"

He let the words hang before shaking his head, laughing.

"Man, you going soft on me, bro. This girl got your head gone."

Vaughn chuckled, but he knew it was true.

The thing was—he didn't care.

He was in love.

Psalm was all he needed. She was his escape from the streets, the only thing keeping him grounded.

Just the thought of her had him floating.

Vaughn shook it off.

"Look, man, I'm out." He dapped Blizz up.

"Y'all niggas make sure that money and dope get put up safely."

Blizz nodded.

"Shit, I'm leaving right behind you. I'll text Sada—tell him to make sure everything gets counted and locked up. He the most trustworthy anyway."

Vaughn and Blizz dapped each other up, then hopped into their cars and parted ways.

But inside, Tec stood on the other side of the door, rubbing his fingers through his beard. He had just heard every word. And that information?

It was worth something.

CHAPTER 12: JETSON'S REVENGE

Jetson sat in his car, gripping a half-empty bottle of Don Julio, the liquor burning a path down his throat.

Murderous thoughts swarmed his mind as he massaged the trigger of his brand-new .38 Special revolver.

His jaw clenched as he glanced at the dashboard clock—three hours had passed since he first parked outside Vaughn's house.

He had done his homework, digging up the address with a little investigating. Now, all that was left was for Vaughn to step outside.
Tonight, Jetson would show him that he wasn't the pussy Vaughn thought he was.

The humiliation from the gas station still burned deep, festering like an untreated wound. Vaughn had stripped him of his manhood in front of Psalm, punking him out like he was nothing.

First, he lost his girl—now, his pride.

He refused to let it slide.

The liquor in his system only fueled his rage, pushing him toward the only resolution he saw fit: Revenge.

Suddenly, the front door creaked open. There he is.

Vaughn stepped outside, phone pressed to his ear, completely oblivious to the danger lurking in the shadows.

Jetson tensed, slumping lower in his seat, pulling his hoodie tight over his head.

His heart pounded as he slid the chamber out of the revolver, double-checking that all the bullets were in place.

Locked and loaded.

His fingers wrapped around the door handle, ready to spring into action.

But just as he prepared to move, a small figure appeared behind Vaughn.

A little girl.

Jewel.

Jetson froze.

Fuck.

His grip tightened on the gun as his mind raced.

Move, little girl. Get the fuck out the way.

As much as he wanted Vaughn dead, he wasn't heartless enough to risk killing an innocent child.

His stomach twisted in frustration as Vaughn and the girl climbed into the car.

Jetson could do nothing but watch as Vaughn backed out of the driveway, completely unaware of how close he had just come to cheating death.

"Fuck!"

Jetson slammed his fists against the steering wheel.

He debated whether to follow Vaughn, wait for a moment when he was alone— But then he saw her.
Psalm.

She stepped outside, walking down the driveway toward the mailbox, completely unaware of his presence.

His lips curled into a wicked grin. Now's my chance.

Taking a final swig from the bottle, he shoved the gun into his waistband and jumped out of the car, moving with purpose.

As Psalm turned back toward the house—he sprinted up the driveway.

Before she could close the door, he was there.

He jammed his foot against the door and slammed his way inside, the force sending Psalm sprawling onto the floor.

A scream escaped her lips, but before she could fully react—he was on her.

Jetson yanked her up by her hair, pressing the cold steel of his gun against her neck. "Bitch, shut the fuck up with all that screaming," he snarled.

Psalm's breath hitched as she stared at him, wide-eyed.

The overwhelming stench of liquor radiated from his breath.

"Jetson, please, don't do this," she pleaded, tears streaming down her face.

He sneered.

"Bitch, don't tell me what the fuck to do."

His voice dripped with venom.

"You didn't say that shit when that nigga had a gun to me!"

His face twisted in fury.

"Nah, I don't wanna hear it!"

Jetson dragged her toward the living room and shoved her onto the couch.

"Sit your ass down!"

Psalm sobbed, trembling as he stood over her, waving the gun wildly. "You left me for him?"
His voice cracked with rage.

"After me and my family took you in? You was out here with nothing before you met me! Sleeping on the fucking streets! And this is how you repay me?"

He paced the room, the gun shaking in his hand.

"I should kill you," he growled.

Psalm sobbed harder.

"I'm sorry, Jetson. Please—"

Smack!

His hand cracked across her face, snapping her head to the side. Pain exploded in her cheek. She gasped.

"Stop fucking telling me what not to do before I do it!"

Psalm knew she had to think fast.

If she didn't fight back now, she was dead.

Jetson pointed the gun at her again, fury blazing in his eyes.

"I'm gonna kill you and that bitch-ass nigga!"

Now or never.

Psalm sprung from the couch, ramming into him like a raging bull.

They slammed into the wall, cracking the drywall as they wrestled for the gun. She clamped her teeth onto his forearm—

Biting down hard, drawing blood.

"AHH, you bitch!" Jetson roared.

She drove her knee into his groin.

Hard.

The gun clattered to the floor.

Kick it away!

She sent it skidding across the room with a powerful kick—but Jetson tackled her, pinning her beneath his weight.

He was heavier, stronger—too strong.

His hands wrapped around her throat.

"Bitch, I'm gonna kill you!"

Psalm gasped, her lungs begging for air as she clawed at his hands—but his grip was relentless.

Black dots danced in her vision.

She was dying.

Her thoughts blurred.

Vaughn…

Then, she saw it.

A gun.

Lying under the TV stand.

With the last of her strength, she stretched her arm, her fingers brushing against cold steel. Got it.

Jetson didn't even see it coming.

BOOM!

The first shot ripped through his stomach.

BOOM! BOOM! BOOM!

Three more shots exploded into his chest.

His eyes widened, his grip loosening.

He gasped, blood bubbling from his lips.

His body collapsed onto her, lifeless.

Psalm sucked in a desperate gulp of air, coughing violently. She shoved him off, rolling onto her side, panting.

She looked down at his open, vacant eyes.

If they die with their eyes open, they deserved it.

Blood stained her shirt.

Her hands trembled as she clutched the gun.

"Thank you, God," she whispered.

Then came the chaos.

Loud booming against the door.

Heavy footsteps.

Shouting.

"FREEZE! DROP YOUR WEAPON!"

Police stormed into the house, guns trained on her.

Psalm stood there, dazed, still holding the smoking gun. Their voices blurred.

"DROP YOUR WEAPON!"

She blinked, her mind sluggish.

Boom. Boom. Boom.

The bullets tore into her. Everything went black.

***

Blizz gripped the Jamaican girl's waist, pounding into her from behind, lost in the moment. "Say you love Daddy's dick," he growled.

She let out a gasp, arching her back, throwing herself against him, her thick ass smacking against his abdomen with loud, wet claps.

His hand came down hard, leaving a red imprint on her caramel skin.

"Ooh, me love Daddy's dick!" she moaned, barely able to speak as she came up for air—her face buried between the thighs of the Spanish girl beneath her.

The Spanish girl moaned in ecstasy, gripping the sheets as her body trembled.

Her juices coated the Jamaican girl's chin, glistening under the dim bedroom light.

Without hesitation, the Jamaican girl dove back between her thighs, flicking her tongue against her swollen clit.

Blizz grinned, reaching for a bottle of Bel-Air champagne.

He took a long swig, then poured it over both women, watching the liquid drip down their bodies, mixing with sweat and liquor.

I'm the fucking man.

Blizz thrust deeper, his ego swelling as the girls moaned his name.

Then—

His phone rang.

Fucking timing.

He reached for the nightstand, still inside the Jamaican girl, and glanced at the caller ID. Vaughn.

With a sigh, he answered.

"Vaughn, what's good, baby?" Blizz said, slightly out of breath.

Vaughn's voice was tight, urgent.

"Yo, I'm at the hospital, man. The fucking police shot Psalm. They got her handcuffed to a bed. This shit is all bad."

Blizz sat up slightly, his mind shifting in an instant.

"Hold on, hold on—what? Slow down, bro. Why the fuck did the police shoot your girl?"

"I don't fucking know, man! That's what I'm trying to figure out." Vaughn's voice was raw, stressed.

"All I know is these cops standing guard outside her room, talking about she's charged with first-degree murder."

Blizz wiped the sweat from his forehead.

"First-degree murder? What the fuck happened?"

Vaughn exhaled hard.

"The neighbor called the police when she saw someone breaking into my crib. When I rode by, I saw Jetson laid the fuck out—dead as a doorknob."

Blizz shook his head.

"Damn, son. That's some crazy shit."

His hand slid back to the Jamaican girl's ass, gripping it absentmindedly.

"Look, Blizz, I know they gonna set her bond. The most it'll be is a million. The bonding company will take fifteen percent of that. Cops told me they'll book her in a few hours." Vaughn took a deep breath.

"I gotta stay here and make sure she's straight. I need you to loan me that $150,000 and take it straight to the bail bondsman. I don't want my girl in jail for a second longer than she has to be."

Blizz hesitated for half a second.

Then—

"Yeah, I got $150K in the safe. You know I got you, family."

The moans of the girls were still loud in the background.

Vaughn noticed.

"Yo, Blizz, I know you havin' a time right now," he said, his voice carrying a dangerous edge.

"But I need you, B. Fuck them bitches. Let's handle this situation."

Blizz smirked, but deep down, he knew Vaughn was right.

"Yeah, that's a fact, Brody. I'm on it. I'll see you in a minute."

"Aight, one."

The call ended.

Blizz tossed the phone onto the nightstand, exhaling.

Then—he turned back to the women.

"Yo, throw that ass back," he commanded, reaching into his robe pocket.

He pulled out a Perc, popped it in his mouth, and washed it down with a swig of Bel-Air. Vaughn could wait.

***

4:00 AM – Suffolk County Jail

Vaughn sat in his car outside the jail, his patience wearing thin. Blizz was nowhere to be found

His phone screen glowed in the darkness.

Fifteen missed calls. No answer.

"What the fuck, Blizz? Where you at, man?!" Vaughn muttered. Psalm had already been booked.

Just like he predicted, the judge set her bond at one million dollars. The problem?

Blizz never showed up with the money.

Vaughn clenched his jaw.

He had his own money, but it was locked away in a safe deposit box, and the bank wouldn't open until 9 AM.

That meant Psalm would have to sit in jail for five more hours—all because Blizz was bullshitting.

His phone sat in his lap, the screen darkening.

He snatched it up and called Blizz again.

Ring. Ring. Ring.

Still no answer.

Vaughn's leg bounced with frustration.

His patience was running thin as fuck.

Ring. Ring.

Finally, after what felt like forever,

The call connected.

A groggy voice mumbled,

"Yo…"

Vaughn's blood boiled.

"Blizz, where the fuck you at, man?!"

Silence.

Blizz yawned.

That was the last straw.

"Don't tell me you fuckin' slept through this, B. I called you fifteen times! Psalm's in jail, nigga!" Blizz groaned, sitting up and rubbing his eyes.

His robe was still open, the two naked women sprawled out beside him.

He blinked at the phone screen, squinting.

"Ah, shit."

Vaughn's voice was pure fury.

"You playin' games with my girl's freedom, B? You think this shit funny?!" Blizz swung his legs off the bed, running a hand down his face.

His Perc haze was still in his system.

"Yo, chill, chill, I got you. I'm on my way right now," he said quickly. Vaughn wasn't buying it.

"Nah. Fuck all that." His voice was ice cold.

"You made me wait out here while you laid up with some bitches? You think I ain't peep that shit in the background when I called you earlier?"

Blizz tried to explain, but Vaughn wasn't hearing it.

"You showed me exactly who you are tonight, nigga. We gonna talk about this later."

Click.

Blizz stared at the phone screen.

For the first time in years, he felt something in Vaughn's voice that he had never heard before. Pure fucking disgust.

And something even worse.

Disrespect.

Blizz shook his head, dragging a hand down his face.

Damn.

He really fucked up.

CHAPTER 13: THE COST OF POWER

Vaughn sat at the minibar in his living room, swirling a glass of cognac as he waited for his crew to arrive.

The meeting wasn't urgent—nothing was wrong. In fact, everything was going smoothly— But he still felt the need to keep his grip tight.

Control was everything.

The Space Jam operation was thriving, and Vaughn wanted to expand.

More bricks.

More corners.

More power.

His thoughts were interrupted by voices echoing inside the house.

The twins, Sada and Blitz, entered first, moving like a two-man wrecking crew.

Vaughn stood up to greet them at the threshold of the living room, dapping them up one by one. "Evening, gentlemen. Everybody take a seat."

They followed his lead as he turned toward Gruff, his towering security detail.

"Mugz, pour these guys a drink."

"You got it, boss," Mugz rumbled, his deep voice like a damn earthquake.

Since Jetson's intrusion, Vaughn had beefed up security, hiring Mugz to keep things tight and handle business around the house.

As Mugz poured drinks, Vaughn stood front and center, looking over his crew.

"Let me start by saying—Space Jam is booming. We got Long Island locked. This shit is on every corner a hustler stands."

The crew clinked glasses, nodding in satisfaction. A few grinned, soaking in the praise. "I salute y'all for playing your part," Vaughn added, taking a sip from his glass.

The room erupted in celebration—fist bumps.

Clapping hands.

Boasting.

"That's what the fuck I'm talking about!"

"Word up, we running this shit!"

Vaughn smirked, but raised a hand.

"Hey, keep it down. Psalm's upstairs resting," he warned.

The room settled.

"Now, I spoke with the plug—he's ready to flood us with more bricks than we can chew." He paused, making eye contact with each of them.

"We're partnering with the Russians from Brooklyn. They dropped their supplier just to fuck with us."

His words hung heavy in the air.

"Mugz, bring the bag."

Mugz, 6'7" of pure muscle, left the room.

Moments later, he returned carrying a small duffel bag. He set it down on the table in front of them.

Vaughn unzipped it.

Inside—50 bricks.

"These belong to the Russians. They already paid up. Now—can I trust you two to get these delivered safely tomorrow night?"

His eyes locked on Blizz and Sada.

Sada nodded instantly.

"Without a doubt."

"Of course," Blizz added.

Vaughn's gaze hardened.

He wanted them to feel the weight of his words.

"No fuck-ups."

Once he was satisfied that they understood, he nodded toward Mugz.

Mugz tossed the duffel bag at them, and it landed between them on the couch.

"That's all for today. If y'all need me, hit my cell," Vaughn dismissed them. One by one, the crew filed out—all except Blizz.

Blizz hesitated, then stepped forward.

"Yo, man, I know you kinda tight with me about the bond situation, but I'ma make sure this gets handled," Blizz said, tapping the duffel bag.

Vaughn didn't flinch.

"Don't tell me. Show me."

Blizz nodded once, then left.

The front door closed shut, leaving Vaughn exhaling deeply.

It wasn't easy being the boss.

He glanced over at Mugz, who stood silently, hands clasped in front of him. "Anything you need, boss?" Mugz asked.

"All the cameras installed? Inside and outside the house?"

"Yes, sir. All up and running."

Vaughn nodded.

"Good. I gotta give Psalm her meds. You can relax for a while."

Mugz gave a small nod, stepping back.

***

Vaughn made his way up the stairs, slowly opening the bedroom door, careful not to wake Psalm.

But to his surprise—she was awake.

Laid back in bed, flipping through TV channels.

"Hey, babe. Thought you were asleep," he said, stepping inside.

She glanced over at him.

"I was, but the pain from the gunshot wounds woke me up."

She had tooken a bullet to her shoulder. A flesh wound, the bullet went in and out. Vaughn pulled her prescription bottle from his pocket.
"I know. Here, take these."

She swallowed the pills and took a sip from her water bottle.

"Thanks, baby," she murmured.

Vaughn sat on the edge of the bed, running his fingers through her hair.

He kissed her softly.

But he wasn't stupid—he noticed the change in her ever since she got out.

She was quiet.

Always in her head.

Maybe it was Jetson's death haunting her.

Maybe it was the case.

Either way, he had already dropped serious money on a top-tier lawyer.

If anyone could get her off on self-defense, it was him.

"How you doing, though, baby? How's your mental?" he asked gently.

Psalm exhaled.

"I don't wanna talk about that right now. How did the meeting go?"

Vaughn sighed.

"Everything went well. I told the guys we're moving with the Russians. They already paid for the bricks, so I put Blizz and Sada in charge of the drop."

Psalm's eyes flickered with something. "Hmm."

Vaughn caught that.

"What? What's wrong with that?"

She looked at him.

"Baby, I don't think you should trust Blizz with that." "Why not?"

"Not trying to talk bad about him, but Blizz is irresponsible. Half the time, his mind is on partying and bitches."

Vaughn knew she was right.

But Blizz needed to prove himself.

"You're right. But this is easy—all he has to do is drop them off." Psalm shook her head.

"It's simple, yeah. But you need to start making better decisions. You're the brains of this operation. So start acting like it."

Vaughn stared at her.

Then, slowly, he nodded.

"You're right."

"And another thing—you need to stop keeping everything here. The money, the drugs—you need a stash house. If the police run up in here, we're both doing time."

Vaughn knew she was right.

"Yeah, I'm tripping. I'ma have the twins set up a spot in Wyandanch." "Good. Now give me a kiss."

He smiled, leaned in, and kissed her.

Then—his phone vibrated.

He pulled it out.

Incoming call: Astoria.

"Hold on, babe, let me take this," he said, stepping into the hallway. He answered.

"Yo."

Astoria's voice hit him like a brick.

"Baby, why haven't you been answering my calls? You promised me if I helped you set those guys up, you'd spend time with me."

Vaughn rubbed his forehead.

"Astoria… I been busy."

Her voice sharpened.

"Is it another bitch?"

Silence.

Then—Vaughn told her the truth.

"Yeah. I got a girl. And I plan on doing right by her."

Silence.

Then—sobs.

"Astoria, I'm sorry."

"No, you're not, nigga! You used me! You're a bitch-ass nigga, and you gonna get yours!" Click.

Vaughn hung up.

He had bigger problems.

CHAPTER 14: SNAKES IN THE SHADOWS

The Stash House

Blizz sat on the sofa, a garbage bag full of cash spread open in front of him.

He reached inside, pulling out thick stacks of big-faced bills, stacking them neatly on the coffee table.

Across the room, Milli stood at the front door, gripping his AK-47 tight, peering through the window every few minutes.

His body was tense.

Paranoia was mandatory in this game.

They had just secured this new stash house, per Vaughn's orders.

The same house where the Wyandanch crew got robbed and killed.

Vaughn took it over—not just to steal their clientele, but to send a message.

There were new kings in town.

And they weren't to be fucked with.

***

In the kitchen, Sada was teaching Tec the finer details of cooking crack in the microwave.

"After I take this bitch out, that mother fucker going to be just right, watch." Sada bragged, adjusting the timer.

Tec grinned.

"Okay, okay, I see you, my nigga," he said, impressed.

Tec walked into the living room, where Blizz was deep in his money count.

"Damn, my nigga, let me help you count some of that cheese," Tec offered, cracking his knuckles.

Blizz didn't even look up.

"Nah, I got this," he said, his fingers never stopping.

Tec's smile faded.

Blizz didn't trust him.

Tec had sheisty energy, and if there was one rule in the streets— Money had to be counted by trusted hands.

"Man, that shit gonna take you all day, you sure?" Tec asked again.

Blizz laughed.

"Yeah, nigga, I'm sure."

Tec sucked his teeth and fell back onto the couch, grabbing the remote and tossing it over to Tec.

"Find you a movie or something to watch. I got this." Said Blizz. "Yeah, aight, suit yourself," he muttered, turning on the TV.

Blizz's phone vibrated on the table.

He grabbed it.

A text from Vaughn.

Lorraine Street in Red Hook. Be there at 9:30. At the bus stop.

Blizz replied back:

Copy.

That was the address for him and Sada to drop off the bricks to the Russians. Blizz was about to stash the money, preparing to leave—then he remembered something.

That fine-ass Cuban chick.

He had met her at the club, and tonight was supposed to be their first link-up. Blizz leaned back, rubbing his chin.

Handle business? Or get some ass?

He made his decision.

Get some ass.

"Yo, Sada!" Blizz called out.

Sada appeared within seconds.

"What's good?"

Blizz stood up.

"I'm about to text you the address for the drop. Make sure you're there at 9:30."

Sada frowned.

"I thought Vaughn said we were supposed to do this together?"

Blizz smirked.

"Yeah, he did. But I'm telling you to handle it solo. You need me to hold your hand, nigga?" Sada expression hardened.

"Nah, I got it."

"Good. If Vaughn asks, tell him I was there."

Tec suddenly jumped up.

"Yo, should I ride with you, Sada?"

Sada shook his head.

"Nah. You and Milli hold this spot down."

Blizz tossed Tec a few ounces of coke.

"Keep packaging this up."

"Aight, bet."

Blizz threw the duffel bag at Sada.

They nodded at each other, then headed out.

***

Astoria sat inside her car, her nails digging into the steering wheel.

She had been watching the stash house all night, waiting for confirmation that it belonged to Vaughn and his crew.

And now—she had it.

Her heart burned with rage.

She had risked her life setting up those niggas for Vaughn, only to get discarded like she meant nothing.

That was the last fucking straw.

She slouched lower in the driver's seat as Two men stepped out of the house.

Then—her eyes widened.

She recognized them from the robbery.

Blizz. Sada.

That was all the confirmation she needed.

She pulled out her phone and snapped a picture of Sada's license plate as he drove away. Her blood boiled.
"I don't give a fuck. Everybody associated with this nigga is going down."

She dialed 911.

A calm voice answered.

"911, what's your emergency?"

"Yeah, I got a tip on a stash house full of drugs, and a car that just left with either a whole lot of dope or a whole lot of money."

She rattled off the address and Sada's plate number, then hung up. "This motherfucker's gonna learn about fucking with me."

***

Sada bopped his head to the music as he cruised down the Long Island Expressway.

He hadn't even been on the road for fifteen minutes when he noticed the black Suburban behind him.

His heart dropped.

Then—red and blue lights flashed.

"Fuck, fuck, fuck!" he cursed, punching the steering wheel.

"Just be cool, Sada. You ain't do shit wrong," he muttered to himself as he pulled over. Two officers approached—one on each side.
Sada rolled down the window and instantly recognized one of them.

Detective Vincent.

The smirking white cop chewed his gum and pulled off his sunglasses.

"Well, well, well. If it ain't you again, Sada."

Sada forced a smile.

"Just been staying out of trouble, man."

Vincent chuckled.

"Yeah? I don't know about that. We've been watching you."

Sada started sweating.

He prayed they wouldn't check the trunk.

Vincent leaned in.

"Step out the car. Let's have a little chat."

Sada hesitated, but complied by stepping out the car.

Then—he ran.

He made it a few feet before—BZZZZZT!

The taser hit his back.

Sada collapsed, his body seizing as volts shot through him.

He screamed in pain as Vincent's knee pressed against his neck.

"Come on, Sada, why you running? That tells me you got something in that trunk."

Vincent patted him on the shoulder.

"Stay put while I take a look."

Moments later, Vincent returned—duffel bag in hand.

He unzipped the bag racing it's contents.

His eyes widened.

"Jesus Christ, Sada. This is a lot of fucking weight."

Vincent smirked.

"You know what that means, right? You're looking at at least twenty-five years."

Sada lowered his head.

"No need to keep talking, nigga. Just take me to jail."

Vincent laughed.

"Nah. I got a better idea."

He pulled out a burner phone and shoved it in Sada's pocket.

"You're gonna tell me everything about Vaughn's operation. When I call, you answer." Sada clenched his jaw.

His life was now in Detective Vincent's hand.

CHAPTER 15: THE BREAKING POINT

Kuzma sat behind his massive oak desk, puffing on a thick Cuban cigar, the smoke curling lazily in the air.

His private office, nestled in the heart of his lavish Brooklyn estate, was guarded by two Russian enforcers, each gripping MP-14s, standing stone-faced and ready for whatever.

Kuzma, the ruthless president of the Russian cartel, ruled the New York underworld with an iron fist.

Their business?

Drugs and violence.

Their reputation?

Feared and respected across all five boroughs.

Kuzma ran his fingers through his salt-and-peppered beard, his mind processing what his runner had just told him.

His short temper was legendary. And right now—his blood was boiling.

"What do you mean they never showed up with the product?" Kuzma growled, staring down the nervous Russian standing before him.

The man swallowed hard, his hands twitching at his sides. He hated being the bearer of bad news.

"We waited at the location you gave us, boss. We stayed an extra two hours, but they never showed. So we left," the man reported, his voice shaky.

Kuzma's face turned red.

His nostrils flared, his breathing grew heavy.

Vaughn had betrayed him.

He had given Vaughn the money up front, trusting him to deliver once the shipment arrived. But now—

Vaughn was MIA, and the product was missing.

A dangerous game to play with a man like Kuzma.

"So you're telling me these niggers played me out of my money?" Kuzma asked, his voice eerily calm.

The Russian lowered his head, knowing what was coming next. "Sir, that's what it seems to look like," he murmured.

Silence.

Then—Kuzma laughed.

A low, menacing chuckle that sent a chill through the room.

His enforcers exchanged uneasy glances, unsure if their boss was finding humor in the situation—

Or calculating murder.

Kuzma leaned back in his chair, exhaling a cloud of cigar smoke. "I can't believe this," he muttered, rubbing his temples.

Then—he stood.

He walked toward the wall behind his desk, where an antique samurai sword hung, its blade gleaming under the dim office lights.

Kuzma took it down, unsheathing it slowly.

The sound of the blade slicing through air made the room even colder.

"These Black niggers want to fuck with me, huh?" Kuzma murmured, pacing.

Then—without warning—he thrust the blade deep into his runner's stomach. "Aghh!"

The man's eyes widened in shock as blood poured from the wound.

His hands grasped at Kuzma's forearm, but the Russian shoved the sword in deeper—his face emotionless.

The man gurgled, his knees buckling.

He tried to breathe, but his lungs failed him.

Kuzma pulled the blade out slowly, watching the man collapse to the floor, twitching. His last breath left his lips.

Still, Kuzma felt no satisfaction.

One death wasn't enough.

He turned to his enforcers, his voice deadly cold.

"You two."

The guards stood at attention.

"Find Vaughn. Kill him. And anybody associated with him. I want his fucking head." The men nodded.

"Now go."

They rushed out to assemble their crew.

Kuzma wiped the blood off his blade, his lips curling into a sinister smirk.

***

Vaughn cruised down Doctor's Path in Riverhead, Psalm in the passenger seat, her long nails tapping against her phone.

The streets were quiet, the city's underbelly buzzing beneath the surface.

Vaughn had been running his rounds, collecting from his hustlers, making sure business was smooth.

But one thing was off—he hadn't heard from Blizz or Sada.

He reached for his phone, dialed Blizz.

Blizz picked up on the first ring.

"Yo," Blizz answered, voice cool.

"What up? Everything go good with that situation I left you in charge of?" Vaughn asked, referring to the Russian drop-off.

Blizz forced a smirk, even though his stomach was knotting up. "Yeah, everything Gucci, Brody," Blizz lied.

In reality, he had been calling Sada all night, but no response.

That wasn't a good sign.

Until he figured it out, he'd let Vaughn believe everything was smooth.

"Bet. Good looking out, bro. You came through for me," Vaughn said.

Hearing that made Blizz feel like shit.

"No problem, my nigga. Anytime," Blizz responded, his voice hollow.

"I'm out here collecting some paper, then me and wifey heading back to the crib. I'll get up with you tomorrow," Vaughn said.

"Aight, bet. Later." Click.

Vaughn turned toward Psalm, grinning.

"What?" Psalm asked, eyeing his expression.

"Blizz did it, baby."

"Did what?"

"Him and Sada. They delivered the package to the Russians. Just like I asked." Psalm's expression darkened.

"I still think he's a fuck-up," she muttered. "You need to drop him."

Vaughn sighed.

"I can't do that, baby. Blizz is like a brother to me."

Psalm rolled her eyes.

"Yeah, I know. But he's a liability."

Vaughn let her words sink in.

He knew she was right—but Blizz was his day-one.

Time would tell.

***

Vaughn pulled up to the corner store.

"Stay here, baby. I'll be right back." He kissed her lips.

Psalm nodded.

"Okay, honey."

Vaughn stepped into the cold New York night, the wind cutting through his hoodie.

Inside he stopped at the counter and greeted Saddiq, the ocki who owned the bodega. "Vaughn, how's it going my friend?" Asked Saddiq

"I can't complain my ock. Just doing my rounds. Yo let me get a plate of chicken over rice. Add extra white sauce." He replied while giving Saddiq some dap.

"Coming right up my brother."

With that being said Vaughn turned on his heels heading to the back of the store where the storage room was.

Inside, he saw Dollar, his hustler.

"Yo, where's my bread?" Vaughn called.

But what he saw froze him in place.

Dollar, pants at his ankles—getting his dick sucked by a crackhead. His mother.

DeeDee.

Vaughn's vision blurred with rage.

BOOM.

His fist crashed into Dollar's face, dropping him.

STOMP. STOMP. STOMP.

Blood splattered the floor.

DeeDee curled into a ball, trembling.

"Please don't hurt me," she whimpered.

She was so high on crack, that she didn't even notice it was her own son doing the damage. Vaughn's stomach twisted in disgust.

He stormed out. Making his way to the front door to exit.

"You don't want your food my friend? It's almost ready." Said Saddiq.

"Naw I'm good" replied Vaughn heading to the exit obviously frustrated.

Then—a black van pulled up.

The side door slid open.

Gunfire erupted.

BOOM! BOOM! BOOM!

Bullets ripped through the store's front windows, shattering glass to the front door.

Vaughn fell back inside, ducking behind the ice cream freezer as bullets tore through the air. He reached for his gun—but it wasn't there.

His stomach dropped.

He had left it in the car with Psalm.

"Psalm! Fuck!" he cursed under his breath, his mind racing with panic.

Outside, gunfire still rained down, the assassins emptying clips into the store.

Then—two of them broke off from the van, creeping toward the entrance, moving in for the kill. Vaughn peeked up just in time to see their silhouettes sliding past the broken glass.

***

"Vaughn, catch!"

Saddiq, the store owner, shouted as he tossed him a Glock—switch attached. Vaughn caught it and lay low, waiting for his moment.

The first gunman crouched inside like a cat, his chopper raised, scanning the store. Too late.

Vaughn sprung from behind the freezer, finger locked on the switch. BRRRRRRTTT!

The Glock spat bullets, tearing through the hitman's chest, ripping his body apart before he even had a chance to react.

He collapsed, his body convulsing as blood pooled beneath him.

The second assassin rushed in, firing wildly.

POP-POP-POP-POP!

Bullets whizzed past Vaughn's head, tearing through bags of chips, exploding soda bottles, sending liquid and debris flying.

Vaughn ducked, his ears ringing from the shots.

Then—Saddiq moved.

From behind the counter, the store owner stood tall, gripping an AK-47.

"ALLAHU AKBAR!" Sadiq roared, unloading a hail of bullets into the second gunman's torso. BANG! BANG! BANG! BANG!

The assassin jerked violently, his body stumbling back before hitting the floor with a sickening thud.

He gasped for air, his life slipping away.

Vaughn stepped forward, standing over the dying man. POP! POP!
Two shots to the head.

Lights out.

Vaughn wasn't leaving loose ends.

***

Vaughn moved toward the entrance—but movement caught his eye.

Outside, another hitman ducked behind a parked car, reloading his weapon. CRACK-CRACK-CRACK!

Three rapid shots were fired in Vaughn's direction.

He dove back, pressing against the wall near the front door.

The shooter was still there.

Vaughn reached around the doorway, blind firing two shots, just enough to keep the shooter in place.

His real focus was on the car.

Psalm was still inside.

"You wanna play? Let's play, motherfucker!"

Vaughn took a deep breath—then broke cover, his Glock singing. BRRRRRTTTT!

The switch-fired bullets ripped through the car, chewing up metal and glass, leaving the hitman scrambling for new cover.

Vaughn backpedaled toward his car, his clip running dry in seconds. Then—the gun fell silent.

Shit. Empty.

Before he could reload—POP! POP! POP!

The gunman jumped from behind an old Nissan, letting off rounds. A bullet sliced through Vaughn's calf.

"Aghhh!"

Pain exploded through his leg, and Vaughn collapsed, clutching his wound. The shooter closed in, his assault rifle aimed, circling Vaughn like a predator. Vaughn stared down the barrel, his breathing ragged.

This was it.

He was out of time.

***

BOOM!

A shot rang out.

The hitman's head snapped back, his body jerking violently before he hit the pavement. Blood spilled onto the concrete, his brains leaking from the exit wound.

Vaughn turned his head—

Psalm stood a few feet away, gun smoking in her hands.

"Baby, get up! We gotta go!" she yelled, running toward him.

She grabbed his arm, struggling to lift him.

"Arghhh," Vaughn grunted, pain shooting through his leg as she helped him to his feet. He hobbled toward the car, leaning on her.
Then—he stopped.

"Hold on," he breathed, his eyes locking onto the dead gunman.

"Take his mask off."

Psalm hesitated, then ripped it away.

Vaughn stared at the lifeless face—he didn't recognize him.

But one thing was clear.

He was Russian.

"Why the fuck is a Russian trying to kill me?"

His mind swirled with a thousand questions.

Psalm grabbed his face, urgency in her voice.

"Baby, we don't have time for this! Cops are gonna be all over this place! We need to leave." Vaughn nodded, gritting his teeth.

With one last look at the chaos they left behind, Psalm helped Vaughn into the car.

Then, they sped off.

Leaving nothing but bullet casings and bodies in their wake.

CHAPTER 16: LOOSE LIPS TIGHT GRIPS

Omega swung his tennis racket with force, sending the ball soaring over the net. The machine fired another one, and he adjusted his stance, perfecting his swing under the warm sun. It was a good day to get some exercise.

His phone vibrated in his pocket mid-strike. He exhaled sharply, gripping the racket as he pulled it out.

"¿Qué pasa?" he answered.

A voice spoke briefly on the other end.

"That's fine. Let her in. I'm at the tennis court," Omega replied before hanging up.

His estate was a monument to power—private tennis court, indoor and outdoor pools, even a personal golf course. Every inch of it was proof of the empire he had built.

The sharp click-clack of high heels echoed against the pavement. He smirked, recognizing the rhythm. Turning, he saw Detective Vega striding onto the court.

"Hello, señorita," Omega greeted, the heat in his gaze unmistakable.

"Hello, Mr. Omega," she replied smoothly, her tone laced with confidence.

She was stunning—five-foot-four without heels, her fitted skirt hugging every curve. Long, jet-black hair cascaded over her shoulders, framing light brown eyes that reminded him of Eva Mendes in All About the Benjamins.

Omega extended his hand for a shake, but the moment she reached out, he pulled her close. Their bodies nearly touched, his eyes burning into hers.

"Why do you walk into my house looking this damn good?" he murmured, voice low and teasing. "Give me one reason I shouldn't take you inside and fuck the Mario coins out of you right now."

Vega smirked, pressing a manicured hand against his chest, pushing back just enough to regain space.

"A good reason?" she mused. "I came to handle business—not to lose all my coins, as tempting as that sounds."

Omega chuckled, pulling a thick envelope from the small of his back and handing it to her.

Vega took it, flipping through the crisp hundred-dollar bills before sliding it into her Prada bag.

"Your boy Vaughn is drawing a lot of heat," she said, her tone shifting to business. "My boss is breathing down my neck—and Grayson's—about getting both you and Vaughn off the streets."

Omega lit a cigar, exhaling a slow stream of smoke. "I figured as much. What do they have on me?"

"No hard evidence. Just hearsay," Vega said. "But there's that text from Ronnie—the one where he said you put a hit on him.

It's not enough to convict you, but Grayson? He's out for blood. He knows—you just need to make sure he can't prove it."

Omega stroked his jaw, thinking. "So, it's just talk. No real case. I don't have shit to worry about."

Vega hesitated before continuing. "Grayson is looking for a weak link. He's trying to flip one of your people."

Omega's expression darkened. "Who?"

"Last night, we got an anonymous tip about drug trafficking. When we responded, guess who we found? Your boy Sada—driving a car loaded with product."

Omega exhaled another cloud of smoke, listening intently.

"Grayson had a plan," she continued. "He told us to take the drugs but not arrest him. Then he handed Sada a burner phone—told him to keep us updated on everything that happens with your operation. We haven't heard from him yet, but… you need to be careful."

Omega rolled his cigar between his fingers. "Sada, huh?"

Vega nodded. "Yeah. You might wanna handle that."

Omega's smirk returned. "Thanks for the tip, mamita. I'll take care of it."

Vega winked. "No problem, papi." She turned on her heel, strutting away.

Before she could leave, Omega grabbed her wrist, pulling her back. Their lips crashed together in a heated kiss. The taste of smoke and danger tangled between them.

Vega's hands fumbled with his belt buckle as he pulled her closer, his grip firm on her waist. His pants dropped to his ankles, revealing his hard length. Without hesitation, she sank to her knees, twisting her hair into a tight bun.

Her lips were warm as she swirled her tongue around the tip, teasing him. Slow, deliberate strokes drove him insane. His head fell back in pleasure as she spat on him, stroking his shaft before taking him deep into her throat.

"Fuck," Omega groaned, gripping the back of her head.

Vega worked her magic, taking her time before picking up the pace, stroking him while sucking greedily. She moaned softly, the vibrations sending shivers through his spine.

"I'm close," he warned.

She took him deeper, sucking harder, determined to drain him completely. With a final thrust, he released, his moan echoing across the empty tennis court.

Vega swallowed, wiping her mouth with the back of her hand before licking her lips. "Mmm… tastes good," she teased. Omega, still in a daze, stood with his pants around his ankles. Vega smirked, patting his still-sensitive length.

"See you later, big fella," she purred, sliding her Fendi shades over her eyes before sauntering off, leaving Omega standing in the middle of the tennis court—dick out, mind racing.

***

Sada lay on his bed, staring at the ceiling fan as it spun in slow circles. His mind was racing, the weight of his predicament pressing down on him like a ton of bricks. He had only two choices—jail or death.

If he cooperated with the police and snitched on Vaughn, he'd be dead before he could even think about spending the money he was making. But if he refused to do what these dirty cops wanted, they'd make sure the judge buried him under the prison. Either way, his future was looking bleak.

Frustrated, he let out a deep sigh and threw his hands over his sweaty face. His nerves were shot.

Ring. Ring. Ring.

The burner phone on his nightstand buzzed violently, its glow cutting through the dim room. He already knew who it was.

Sada reached over, snatched the phone, and pressed accept.

"Sada, my main man. How you doing today, brother?" Detective Grayson's raspy voice slithered through the speaker.

Sada sat up, his jaw tightening. "First off, I ain't your brother, motherfucker. Let's get that straight right now." His voice dripped with venom. "Now what the fuck do you dirty-ass pigs want from me?"

Grayson chuckled, but there was no humor in it. "You know exactly what the fuck we want, homeboy. We want Vaughn and Omega's heads on a silver platter. And you are going to be the piece of shit that hands them over."

Sada clenched his fists.

"We need hardcore evidence," Grayson continued. "I'm talking video or audio proof of the operation Vaughn is running for Omega. So here's what you're gonna do." He paused for effect. "Me and Detective Vega are already on our way to your ass right now. We're giving you a wire, and you're gonna wear it. I don't care if it's in person or over the phone, but you better get Vaughn to say something incriminating—or I swear to God, I'll make sure you rot in a cell until your grandkids die of old age."

Sada sucked his teeth and slammed the phone down.

His heart pounded as he sat on the edge of the bed, gripping his head in his hands. The walls were closing in, and the clock was ticking.

He didn't have a choice.

CHAPTER 11: SEED OF DOUBT

Psalm sat cross-legged on the sofa, wearing one of Vaughn's oversized T-shirts, a bowl of ice cream in her lap as she flipped through channels. The TV played in the background, but her mind was somewhere else.

Vaughn was still in the hospital, recovering from a gunshot wound to the leg, but he was expected to be released at any moment. She should have been by his bedside, but he had ordered her to stay away—just in case the Russians decided to come back and finish the job.

Even with the distraction of the TV, Psalm couldn't shake her thoughts of him. She had fallen in love with Vaughn—everything about him. The way he talked, the way he carried himself, the power he exuded. He commanded respect without having to ask for it. His voice, deep and smooth, sent shivers down her spine. The way he moved, so confident, so sure of himself—it turned her on without him even trying.

Her fingers absentmindedly trailed down her stomach, slipping beneath the hem of the T-shirt. She pressed gently against her swollen clit, rubbing slow circles with her middle and ring fingers. A soft gasp left her lips as she slid a finger inside herself, imagining it was Vaughn's tongue, teasing her, making her body tremble. She was right on the edge, her breath coming in short, shallow gasps, when—

Knock! Knock!

The doorbell rang, followed by loud banging on the door.

Psalm growled in frustration. "This some hating-ass shit," she muttered, yanking her hand away and grabbing the .380 handgun from the coffee table.

"Who is it?" she called, agitation clear in her voice. "It's Tec," a voice answered from the other side.

Psalm rolled her eyes, unlocking the door and swinging it open. She stood in the doorway with her hands on her hips, visibly irritated.

"Damn, shorty. You alright?" Tec asked, sensing her energy. "I'm fine. What's up? Did V send you?"

"As a matter of fact, he did." Tec held up a duffle bag and handed it over. "That's 250K from one of the spots."

Psalm took the bag, nodding. "Thanks."

"No problem, ma." Tec smiled, his eyes lingering on her longer than they should. He took in her thick caramel legs, the way the oversized shirt barely covered the curve of her ass.

"Yo, before I go, you mind if I use your bathroom real quick?" he asked.

Psalm hesitated. Something about Tec's energy felt off, but he held up his hands. "One minute, I swear."

"Alright. Down the hall, second door on the right," she instructed before heading back to the sofa. She tucked the gun between her legs beneath the T-shirt—just in case.

A few moments later, Tec emerged from the hallway, lingering in the living room. "What you watching?" he asked casually.

Psalm shot him a glare. "If you don't get the fuck out of my house before Vaughn comes back and kills us both—"

Tec smirked, watching the way her body moved as she walked past him to open the front door. "You think he's untouchable, huh?" Tec thought to himself. "I'll put that little nigga in the dirt." He stepped outside, but before leaving, he turned back to face her.

"You a real one, Psalm. Smart. Bad as hell. And loyal as fuck," he said, his tone sincere. "But I hate to see you being loyal to your enemy."

Psalm frowned. "My enemy? The fuck you talking about?"

Tec shook his head. "You ever find out what happened to your uncle Ronnie?"

Her breath caught in her throat. She hadn't thought about her uncle in a while, but the mention of his name hit her like a freight train.

"No," she admitted softly, a lump forming in her throat.

"Ask Vaughn and Blizz," Tec said. "They know."

Her heart pounded.

"You're lying," she whispered, eyes searching his face. "How do you know this?"

Tec grabbed her hand, lowering his voice. "One day, we were all at the trap spot, and I overheard some—"

Headlights swept across the driveway, cutting him off. Vaughn had arrived.

Mugz helped him out of the car, a crutch under his arm to support his injured leg. Tec immediately stepped toward him, greeting him with a firm hug.

"I'm glad you still here, boss. Don't worry about a motherfucking thing—we gon' kill all those bitches who tried to make a move on you," Tec said, voice filled with conviction.

"Good looking out, family," Vaughn replied, nodding. "You just now dropping that off?"

"Yeah, everything's there," Tec assured him.

"Aight, bet. Yo, tell the family—mandatory meeting tomorrow at 2 PM. I want everyone there." "Say no more," Tec said. "Get well, boss. Peace."

Before getting in his car, Tec made eye contact with Psalm one last time.

She was frozen in place, her mind reeling.

Could it be true?

Vaughn kissed her lips as he stepped inside. "Hey, baby."

"Hey," she replied, her voice distant.

She shut the door behind him, staring at the duffle bag in her hands, her heart pounding.

The truth was out there, and she was about to get to the bottom of it.

CHAPTER 18: NO LOOSE ENDS

Sada sat at the edge of the hotel bed, his leg bouncing as Special Agent Coleman pressed a wire onto his chest.

"Try not to move too much," the agent warned. "The mic picks up everything."

Detective Grayson leaned against the dresser, arms crossed. "Yeah, and we need this scumbag on tape. One good admission, and we've got him." He smirked. "And make sure you bring up Omega's name. That conspiracy charge will stick like glue."

Sada frowned. "Man, hell no. I ain't feeling this shit." He stood up, rubbing his chest like he could will the wire off his body.

Grayson pulled his pistol and pressed the barrel to Sada forehead. "You better have a change of heart. Fast. 'Cause the way I see it, you don't have a choice—unless you want a bullet in your brain."

Sada locked eyes with him, nostrils flaring, fists clenching. "Good." Grayson grinned. "I thought you'd see it my way."

Sada exhaled, his shoulders slumping. "Either way, I'm dead. If Vaughn and Blizz find out I'm wearing this wire, I'm not making it out that meeting today."

"That's why they won't find out," Detective Vega cut in.

Sada sucked his teeth. "Man, you don't know that for sure. Anything could go wrong. And what the hell am I supposed to tell them about the work you took?"

Grayson shrugged. "Tell 'em you got robbed. That's your problem, not mine. Now get your fat ass out of my face and make Vaughn talk."

Sada turned toward the door.

"Hey, don't forget this." Vega tossed him a burner phone from the nightstand.

Sada caught it without looking and stormed out, leaving the door wide open.

As soon as he was gone, Vega glanced at Grayson. "You think he'll go through with it?"

Grayson lit a cigarette, exhaling slowly. "He better. 'Cause I'm the motherfucker he needs to be afraid of, not Vaughn."

"Right," Vega muttered. She turned on her heel. "Excuse me, I need to use the ladies' room." Once inside, she pulled out her personal phone and typed a message:

Sada agreed to cooperate. There's your heads-up.

She hit send. The message went straight to Omega.

Snapping her phone shut, she straightened her shirt and walked back out as if nothing had happened.

***

Sada gripped the steering wheel as he sped down the Long Island Expressway toward Vaughn's crib in Coram. Sweat soaked through his shirt, his stomach twisted in knots.

"Fuck!" he yelled, slamming his fist against the dashboard.

How the hell did it come to this? He'd turned into the very thing he swore he'd never be—a rat. A snitch.

His mind raced. Jail or hell. Life or death. Him or Vaughn.

And the worst part? He actually liked Vaughn. The man had changed his life, given him a real shot. But this was the game. Betrayal came with the territory.

His phone rang. Vaughn.

Sada swallowed hard and answered. "Yo, what's up, boss?"

"Where you at?"

"I'm on the way. Less than ten out."

"Cool. Everybody should be pulling up around the same time. See you in a minute." The line went dead.

Sada clenched his jaw. Tears welled in his eyes. He felt like Judas, ready to betray the man who had only ever looked out for him.

"Nah, fuck that."

With one swift motion, he reached inside his shirt and ripped the wire off. Rolling down the window, he tossed it onto the highway. Then he grabbed the burner phone and hurled it out after it.

"Death before dishonor. Them pigs gotta do what they gotta do."

He had no idea how Vaughn would react to the missing shipment, but that was a problem for later.

***

Vaughn sat at the head of the long dining table, his gaze sweeping across the room. Tec and Milli sat across from him, their expressions unreadable. To their right, Sada and Blizz. Beside Vaughn sat Psalm, her arms crossed, while Mugz stood behind him, silent as ever.

Vaughn laced his fingers together and leaned back. "Anybody know why I called this meeting?" Silence.

"Oh, so everybody quiet now?" He chuckled, but there was no humor in it. "Alright, let's start here—why the fuck do I have Russians trying to execute me in broad daylight?"

Blizz's head snapped up. "Hold on—the Russians were behind that?"

Vaughn nodded slowly. "That's what I just said."

Blizz glanced at Sada, suspicion flickering in his eyes. "The shipment… did you—"

Sada cut him off. "I'll tell you exactly what happened." He took a breath. "Blizz put me in charge of delivering the package."

Blizz's jaw tightened. His glare could've cut through steel.

"That true?" Vaughn asked.

Blizz shrugged. "Yeah, that's true. I made a boss call. What's the problem?" Sada kept going. "The package never got delivered."

Tec scoffed. "Because this greedy motherfucker stole it."

"Man, shut the fuck up," Sada snapped. "I don't gotta steal shit." He turned back to Vaughn. "The cops took it. Grayson and Vega. Dirty-ass detectives."

Vaughn tapped his fingers on the table, absorbing the information.

So that's why the Russians came for him. They thought he was on some bullshit. "So they took the work… and let you walk?"

"They wanted me to flip on you. Said they're building a case on you and Omega. Threatened me with life in prison." Sada shook his head. "But fuck them. I ain't no rat. After everything you've done for me? I could never do that."

Silence stretched across the room.

Vaughn nodded. "I respect your honesty."

Sada exhaled, relieved. "For real, man, I—"

Vaughn snapped his fingers.

No one saw Mugz move, but suddenly, the barrel of a shotgun pressed against Sada's back. BOOM.

The blast shook the room. Sada's eyes widened in shock as blood and bone sprayed across the floor. His body slumped forward, his final breath escaping in a wet, gurgling gasp.

Vaughn stared at the lifeless corpse. "Now I don't gotta worry about whether I can trust him or not."

Omega had made the call anyway for Vaughn to take him out. Silence.

Then, Vaughn turned to Blizz.

"Now… back to you."

Blizz shot to his feet, knocking his chair over. "Nah, you ain't about to talk to me like I'm some kid in front of everybody."

Vaughn leaned forward. "You had one job, and you fucked it up. I almost got killed because of you."

Blizz scoffed. "I made a boss call."

"You ain't no fucking boss. You're a liability."

Blizz's face twisted with rage. "Who put this shit together? Who took care of business when you ain't have the heart to? Me. Blizz." He jabbed a finger at his chest. "I built this shit with you, and this the thanks I get? Man, fuck this family. And fuck you."

He turned and stormed toward the door.

Vaughn seethed, grabbing his water glass and hurling it against the wall. It shattered into a thousand pieces.

"Fuck Blizz," he spat. "And that goes for anybody else who got a problem with it."

CHAPTER 19: BETRAYAL IN THE DARK

"Lil Momma, where you at? We about to start this movie without you." Vaughn called out from the movie room.

Every Sunday night, it was the same routine—him, Jewel, and Psalm curled up together watching movies. Jewel had come up with the tradition herself after she moved in with Vaughn, and they stuck to it ever since.

"No! Don't start it yet, here I come!" Jewel's small voice echoed down the stairs as she rushed into the room, clutching her baby doll and her favorite blanket.

"I had to get my things. Sorry, guys," she said, hopping onto the loveseat between Vaughn and Psalm.

"Yeah, 'cause we was about to start without you. Right, baby?" Vaughn teased, glancing at Psalm.

"We sure was," she murmured, eyes glued to her phone.

Vaughn noticed. The way Psalm had been acting lately—it wasn't like her. She'd been distant, short with him, her answers clipped, her energy different. He could feel something was wrong, but she wasn't letting on.

Psalm knew he sensed the shift, but she didn't care. Her mind was too clouded. She didn't know what to believe.

Could Vaughn really have killed her uncle? The thought alone made her stomach turn.

Ronnie was the only man who had ever truly loved her, and if Vaughn had anything to do with his murder... she didn't even want to finish that thought. She looked over at him, watching as he tickled Jewel, making her cry tears of laughter.

She had to get to the bottom of this. Fast.

Flipping through her contacts, she found Tec's number and typed out a message. - Yo?
Not even twenty seconds later, her phone vibrated.

- What's up, ma ma?

- Can we talk?

- Yeah, but not on the phone. Pull up to the stash spot in Wyandanch.

- Be there in shortly.

She locked her screen. Now she just had to come up with an excuse to leave. "Babe, can you run upstairs and grab me some ice cream?" she asked Vaughn.

"You know you ate the last of it the other night," he reminded her, still wrestling playfully with Jewel.

"Oh yeah, I forgot. Well, Jewel, do you want some ice cream while we watch the movie?" Jewel's face lit up. "Yesss! Butter pecan!"

Psalm smiled as Jewel broke free from Vaughn's hold and started delivering playful punches to his arm.

"Alright, I'm gonna run to the store real quick and be right back." She snatched her car keys from the nightstand and made her way to the door.

"Ayo, bring me some Russian Crème Backwoods and a pack of Now and Laters," Vaughn called out just before she slammed the door shut.

Psalm got in her car and drove, pressing the gas harder than usual. She was nervous, anxious. But most of all, she was determined to know the truth.

Psalm pulled into the driveway of the trap house, her pulse pounding harder than the bass in her speakers. Dressed in Tweety Bird pajamas, Ugg boots, a tank top, and a bonnet, she knew she looked wild—but even on an off night, she still looked good.

She climbed out, slammed the door shut, and marched toward the entrance. Her hand barely reached for the knob before the door swung open.

"Come in," Tec said, stepping aside.

Psalm walked in, her eyes sweeping the living room, instincts kicking in. "Anybody else here?"

"Nah, just me and you," Tec said, locking the door behind her. "Milli just left to check on one of the spots. So, what do I owe this late-night visit?"

Psalm followed him into the kitchen, arms crossed. "I want to know everything." Her tone was like steel.

Tec studied her, then nodded. "Aight. But first, let me pour you a drink. You're gonna need it."

He grabbed two glasses from the cabinet, filling them both with Hennessy before sliding one across the counter. Then, he lifted his own.

Psalm scoffed. "Nah, this ain't no toast. The fuck wrong with you? Start talking." She threw the shot back, welcoming the burn in her throat.

Tec chuckled and downed his drink. "Aight, so boom. One day, we went on a move—me, Milli, Sada, Blizz, and Vaughn. We hit some Wyandanch niggas and took their shit over. Some bitch named Astoria set it up. You know her?"

"Astoria?" Psalm frowned. "Naw, I don't know who the fuck that is. What's that got to do with my uncle?"

"Nothin'. Just asking." He poured them both another shot.

Psalm slammed her hand on the counter. "Na, how do you know Vaughn and Blizz killed my uncle? Get to the point."

Tec smirked. He loved seeing her like this—spitting fire, her energy all sharp edges. "Relax, Lil Momma. I'm getting there."

She clenched her jaw, nostrils flaring, then the back another shot.

"Aight," Tec continued, voice low, deliberate. "So when we got back to the spot, I overheard Blizz and Vaughn talking about the murder."

Psalm's chest tightened.

"They was saying how they handled Ronnie at the block party last year. Blizz told Vaughn not to tell you shit. I heard it with my own ears, ma. They did that shit."

Tears welled in her eyes, but she refused to let them fall. "I don't believe you."

Tec shook his head. "You do. You just don't wanna accept it. But think about it—didn't Vaughn start getting real money right after that block party? Didn't they come up outta nowhere?"

Psalm swallowed hard. "What if they didn't know Ronnie was my uncle? Me and Vaughn weren't even together yet."

Tec leaned in, his voice dropping, heavy with meaning. "Come on, shorty. Don't be stupid. Of course, they knew. Why you think Vaughn pursued you so hard after the murder? That nigga been playing you from day one."

Psalm stared at him, her world tilting, spinning. "You sleeping with the enemy, ma."
The words hit like a gut punch.

Her breath shuddered, her fingers curling into fists. She wanted to scream, to break something, to hurt something.

"I'ma kill them motherfers," she whispered, voice shaking.

Then she broke down like a baby, letting her emotions get the best of her.

Tec moved closer, his arms wrapping around her, firm and steady. "Shhh, it's okay, ma. I got you."

Psalm melted into his hold, her body betraying her as the warmth of his presence overpowered the cold inside her.

She pulled back slightly, looking up at him, her vision blurred. "Thank you, Tec, for—" "Shhh." He cut her off, pressing a finger to her lips.

She stared into his dark eyes.

The air between them shifted.

Maybe it was the liquor. Maybe it was the pain, the betrayal, the anger roaring in her veins.

Or maybe it was just him—his smooth mocha-brown skin, the way his neatly twisted dreads framed his face, the confidence in his stance.

Then he kissed her.

And she let him.

Lips locked, bodies pressing together, her mind drowning in the heat of the moment.

She should've stopped.

She didn't.

She couldn't.

Because right now, Tec wasn't the enemy.

Vaughn was.

And she was about to fuck his opp.

Her body burned, her mind spun, an electric storm of betrayal and lust colliding inside her.

Tec's hands traveled down, gripping her waist before sliding lower, cupping her ass through her pajama shorts. He lifted her onto the counter effortlessly, spreading her thighs as he positioned himself between them.

"You sure you want this, ma?" he murmured against her lips. Her breath was shaky, her nails digging into his shoulders.

"I don't care," she whispered.

That was all Tec needed.

He pulled her panties aside and pushed two fingers inside her, slow but deep, curling them just right.

Psalm gasped, her head falling back against the cabinet.

"That's it, baby," Tec muttered, his lips trailing down her neck. "Let that nigga go. Let me show you how you 'posed to be handled."

She whimpered, her body arching into his touch. His other hand grabbed a fistful of her bonnet, yanking her head up, forcing her to look at him.

"Keep them eyes on me," he ordered.

She obeyed, her breathing ragged as his fingers worked her over, stroking a fire inside her that had nothing to do with love—just pure, reckless rage.

This wasn't about sex.

This was about power.

And Vaughn?

This was gonna destroy him.

***

They sat in silence afterward.

Psalm, still perched on the counter, wrapped in nothing but Tec's oversized hoodie, her body still tingling, her mind an absolute mess.

What the fuck did I just do?*

She bit her lip, staring down at the floor.

Tec watched her, smirking as he lit a blunt, exhaling slow.

"That was some real get-back pussy," he muttered, taking a pull.

Psalm shot him a glare, snatching the blunt from his fingers and taking a deep hit herself.

"I ain't do this for revenge," she lied.

Tec chuckled, his eyes knowing. "Yeah, aight."

He knew the saying oh so well, "a shoulder to cry on, is a dick to ride on."

She exhaled, watching the smoke swirl in the air like the storm brewing inside her.

"Now what?" she asked.

Tec leaned against the counter, arms crossed. "Now? We move smart. You want Vaughn dead?" Psalm hesitated.
She did.

But she wanted something more first.

"No," she said. "Not yet. I want the plug."

Tec raised a brow. "Omega?"

She nodded. "The one that put the hit on Ronnie. I want him."

Tec smirked. "That's cold, ma. I like it."

Psalm turned to him, her expression unreadable. "Can you set it up?"

Tec let the blunt hang from his lips, considering her for a long moment.

Then he nodded. "Yeah. I got you."

She exhaled, some of the weight lifting from her chest.

Good.

Because by tomorrow night, somebody was gonna pay.

Psalm pulled Tec's hoodie tighter around her as she stepped outside, the night air biting against her flushed skin. Her heart was still racing, her mind clouded with everything that had just happened.

Tec followed her to the door, leaning against the frame as he watched her.

"You good?" he asked, his voice low, unreadable.

Psalm nodded, but she couldn't meet his eyes.

She needed to get the fuck out of here before she lost whatever grip she had left on her sanity.

Tec smirked, grabbing her wrist and pulling her into a hug. He held her close, his arms firm, his scent wrapping around her like a trap she knew she shouldn't have stepped into.

Then he tilted her chin up and kissed her again—slow, deep, like he was marking her. And Psalm let him.
Because at that moment, she didn't know what else to do.

When he pulled back, he brushed a thumb over her lips, studying her.

"See you soon, ma."

Psalm swallowed hard and nodded before slipping out of his grip. She hurried to her car, hands shaking as she dug for her keys.

She didn't see the other car parked across the street.

Didn't see the flash of a camera going off behind the tinted windows.

Didn't see Astoria, sitting low in the driver's seat, smirking as she scrolled through the photos on her phone.

Astoria licked her lips, satisfied.

"Got you, bitch."

She took one last picture—Psalm in Tec's hoodie, her face twisted with regret as she pulled off.

CHAPTER 20: ORDERS & CONSEQUENCES

Blizz cruised down Middle Country Road, the bass from Fivio Foreign's new album, Pain and Love 2 rattling the car. Smoke swirled inside, the air conditioner pushing it around, mixing with the thick scent of burning Backwoods.

He flicked the ash into the tray and took a sharp left onto Homestead Drive, pulling into Oakview Apartments—one of the trap spots he and Vaughn ran.

Rolling into a parking space, he let the Scat Pack idle, confident nobody would dare test him. He popped a Percocet dry before washing it down with a quick sip of water, then tossed the bottle to the floor.

Approaching the apartment, he knocked twice.

Within seconds, the door creaked open.

Fatback stood firm in the doorway, arms crossed.

"Yo, what's good?" Blizz said, giving him dap.

"What up?" Fatback replied, his face unreadable.

Blizz noticed something was off. The energy felt wrong.

"Man, fuck out the way, nigga," Blizz said, his face twisting in irritation.

Fatback didn't budge. Instead, he folded his arms tighter. "Got orders from Vaughn not to let you in. Said you ain't family no more."

Blizz stared at him for a moment. Then he laughed.

"Y'all niggas acting like I'm not the fuckin' boss too. I started this shit, nigga!"

"I'm just taking orders, dog. Take that up with Vaughn."

Blizz licked his lips and nodded slowly. "Say that my nigga, I'm out."

He turned on his heels.

But before Fatback could even close the door—

BANG!

A single shot rang out.

A hot one split Fatback's forehead, sending his heavy body crashing to the floor.

Blizz stepped over him like a doormat, gun drawn, as he walked into the tiny apartment.

A worker sitting on the couch, PlayStation controller still in his hands, froze—his eyes wide with terror.

Blizz fixed the gun on him. "I know you into playing games, my nigga, but this ain't one." He waved the pistol. "So, I'ma say this once, and I hope I don't gotta repeat myself. Go grab every piece of dope and every dollar y'all got in this motherfucker. And nothing better be short."

The worker scrambled off the couch, damn near tripping over his own feet as he ran up the stairs.

Blizz sat down, gun still in hand, watching the clock.

Two minutes later, the worker came stumbling back down, lugging two black duffle bags. He dropped them at Blizz's feet.

"How much in here?" Blizz asked.

"Eight bricks of coke and… I'm guessing a little over three hundred thousand."

Blizz nodded. "Word." He slung one duffle over his shoulder, then grabbed the other, heading toward the door.

But he stopped in his tracks, turning back to the terrified man.

"I thought I said I wanted every dollar in this motherfucker."

The worker swallowed hard. "Word to my mother, that's all that's in here."

Blizz squinted, jaw tightening.

"You must not know this a robbery, bitch-ass nigga. What's that in your pocket?"

The man hesitated, eyes darting toward the exit. Slowly, he reached into his front pocket and pulled out a personal bankroll.

Blizz snatched the cash from his hands. BOOM!

A bullet ripped through the worker's stomach, folding him instantly. His body hit the ground with a heavy thud, blood pooling around him.

"That's for not following directions, pussy."

Blizz stepped over his body and glanced back.

"And tell Vaughn I came through. I'm on whatever he on."

With that, he walked out, hopped into his still-running Scat Pack, and peeled off.

CHAPTER 21: BLOOD ON THE BRIDGE

Vaughn, Tec, and Milli sat in a car outside a vacant building in Long Island City, Queens. The word on the street was that this was one of the Russians' drug spots.

Those motherfuckers had made an attempt on Vaughn's life—so now it was only right they sent a message back.

Vaughn could've sat this one out, especially while still recovering from his injury, but his mind was made up. He wanted all the smoke.

"Yo, son, it's been almost four hours we been staking this shit out. You sure this the right spot?" Tec asked, shifting in his seat.

"Yeah, this the right spot, nigga. Matter fact, look—here go some of them motherfuckers coming out right now. What I tell you?" Vaughn said, eyeing three Russian men walking toward a green Tahoe.

He watched them like a lion locking onto prey before going in for the kill.

Tec grabbed his mask, ready. "What's up? We doing 'em in right now?"

"Nah, not right here. Too many cameras," Vaughn whispered.

Milli sat in the back, an AR-15 resting across his lap, silent as always. He didn't talk much, but everyone knew he was always on go.

Vaughn pulled the car into gear. "I got a plan."

***

They trailed the Tahoe, making a left onto 21st Street, heading toward the Queensboro Bridge. Vaughn kept a safe distance, careful not to tip them off.

He pulled out his phone and dialed.

"Mugz, you still in position?"

"Yeah, I'm right outside the Queensbridge Projects," Mugz responded. "Good. You should see the mark soon—it's a green Tahoe."

"Yeah, I spot 'em now," Mugz confirmed.

Right on cue, Mugz pulled out in front of the Tahoe, forcing them onto the expressway leading to the Queensboro Bridge.

They drove further onto the bridge until Mugz suddenly hit the brakes, coming to a dead stop. The Russians slammed on their horn, cursing and yelling.

They didn't even see it coming.

***

Vaughn, Tec, and Milli pulled up alongside the Tahoe.

Vaughn rolled his window down, Glock 23 already out, a 30-round extended clip hanging from the bottom.

Tec climbed halfway out of the passenger-side window. Two twin Smith and Wesson's barking, bullets shredding into the car.

Milli lowered the backseat window, the AR-15 poking out. He let off shots, but that wasn't enough for him—he wanted to feel the action.

He kicked open the back door, stepping out onto the bridge mid-shootout. Planting his stance, he let off rounds like a soldier in combat, turning the Tahoe into Swiss cheese.

Click.

His gun ran empty.

Milli hopped back inside the car.

Vaughn took one last look at the wreckage.

The three Russians were slumped over, bodies twisted over each other, blood leaking into the seats.

Message sent.

Without hesitation, they pulled off, vanishing into the city lights.

***

Inside the safe house, they dropped their guns into a duffle bag.

"Here, Tec. You know what to do with them," Vaughn said, handing him the bag.

Tec smirked, arrogance flashing across his face. "You know what to do with them too. Why you can't go do it yourself?"

"Because I'm telling you to do it, nigga. That's why," Vaughn shot back.

Tec's smirk twitched. Every part of him wanted to slump Vaughn right then and there. He wasn't the type to let just anybody talk to him crazy.

But he played it cool.

He'd wait for the right moment to rock Vaughn to sleep.

"My bad, I'm trippin'. You right, boss," Tec said, grabbing the duffle and walking out. Vaughn watched him leave, then turned to Milli.

"The fuck was that about?"

Milli shrugged. He knew how hotheaded his twin brother was.

But despite Tec's jealousy, Milli was loyal to Vaughn.

He appreciated the opportunity Vaughn had given them— and switching up wasn't in his character.

Milli was official.

"Yeah, I don't know neither. That nigga been acting real funny lately," Vaughn muttered, shaking his head. "I'ma let it go, though. I got too much going on. Blizz just hit one of my spots and killed one of our workers. Now I gotta handle this mf."

Vaughn poured himself a shot of Don Julio.

Milli stood up, cocking his gun, giving Vaughn that look.

"Nah, Milli. Don't worry about it—I'll take care of him," Vaughn said. That's why he loved Milli.

He was a loyal soldier.

Suddenly, footsteps echoed down the stairs.

Psalm appeared. Her face streaked with tears.

She walked into the kitchen, where Vaughn, Milli, and Mugz were posted.

"Can I talk to you for a minute?" she asked Vaughn.

"Yeah, for sure. Yo, Ima holla at you tomorrow," he told Milli.

Milli dapped him up and walked out.

Mugz stayed put, arms folded.

"It's cool, Mugz. Take a break, let me talk to my shorty," Vaughn said.

Mugz nodded and stepped out.

As soon as they were alone, Psalm grabbed both of Vaughn's hands, her eyes full of pain.

"Did you have anything to do with my uncle Ronnie getting killed?" she asked, voice trembling. "And please don't lie to me, Vaughn."

Vaughn froze.

The words got stuck in his throat.

That was all the confirmation she needed.

Her face crumbled as she broke down in tears. "Vaughn, I can't believe you… You been playing in my face this whole time. And you wasn't even gonna tell me."

"Baby, listen— I was gonna tell you. I just didn't know how. I was afraid of losing you," Vaughn pleaded.

"Well, you definitely lost me now."

Her expression hardened. "You're not to be trusted, you snake-ass bitch."

Psalm turned and stormed upstairs to pack her things.

Vaughn followed. "Listen, Psalm, let me explain—"

She spun around, fire in her eyes.

"When those cops pulled us over, you knew exactly what they were talking about, didn't you?!" Her voice cracked.

"You saw how stressed I was, trying to find out who killed my uncle. And you said nothing!" Vaughn stayed silent.

Psalm's face twisted in disgust. "I was staring at the murderer the whole time."

"I didn't kill your uncle, Psalm."

"Then who did?"

Silence.

Vaughn couldn't break the code. He couldn't tell her Blizz pulled the trigger.

She stared at him, waiting.

Nothing.

"You a real foul-ass nigga."

She stuffed her clothes into a suitcase.

Psalm stormed past him, dragging her luggage toward the front door.

SMACK!

Her hand cracked across his face, knocking spit from his mouth.

"You're done to me. And I want you to know—what goes around, comes around, motherfucker. You gon' get yours."

Psalm stormed out, slamming the door shut.

She knew now.

And if the police couldn't get justice for Ronnie...

She would.

Street Justice.

Vaughn just became her next target.

CHAPTER 22: THE WARNING

Vaughn threw back a shot of Hennessy on the rocks, sitting at a round table in the back of his favorite sports bar, watching LeBron James work his magic against the Golden State Warriors.

This was where he came to clear his mind—to think.

His life was in shambles, and he needed a plan to put the pieces back together.

The business was still thriving, money was flowing, and Space Jam still had the streets in a chokehold.

But for how long?

Vaughn knew everything good had to come to an end—especially with this new beef boiling with the Russians.

Going to war meant bodies and losses.

Bodies brought police attention.

And since Vaughn had just sent a message to Kuzma, retaliation wasn't far behind. The only one who could put a stop to this was Omega.

He had connections to everyone who mattered in New York and had been respected since back in the day.

Vaughn made a mental note to inform Omega about his problem with the Russians. But what was really on his mind? Psalm.

Three months had passed since he last spoke to her. She had changed her number, cut off all her contacts—completely erased him from her life.

His heart mourned for her. The way he missed her was unbearable. She was his other half, his soulmate, the yin to his yang.

What was a king without his queen? He had fucked up—bad.

He had to find her and make things right. The family he had worked so hard to build was slowly falling apart.

**

"Don't think too hard, youngin'. You study long, you study wrong."

Vaughn snapped out of his thoughts as Aziz wiped the table with a cloth and placed another shot of Hennessy in front of him.

"As-salamu alaykum, Vaughn," he greeted in Arabic.

"Wa alaikum as-salam," Vaughn replied. He wasn't Muslim, but he had picked up a little from Aziz over the years.

Aziz owned the sports bar and had been in the neighborhood for decades.

He had watched Vaughn grow from a boy into the man he was today—and he was proud of him.

Aziz was like a father figure to many young Black men in the hood, always trying to guide them onto the right path.

"Seems like you got a lot on your mind, kid," Aziz said, taking a seat next to him.

"I do, man. Life's just a little crazy right now, you know? I'm just tryna think of my next move." "Yeah, I know how it can be. Just make sure your next move is your best move, you hear?" "Nah, fasho."

Aziz took a deep breath. "How's your mother doing?"

Vaughn's face darkened, his eyes shifting off the screen.

That said everything.

Aziz sighed. He knew what that meant. She was still getting high.

Aziz and Dee Dee had gone to high school together. They were close once—until Dee Dee started messing with a big-time drug dealer.

Eventually, she got turned out. And that was the beginning of her downfall. Aziz chuckled as he reminisced.

"Man, I remember back in the day like it was yesterday. It was summertime—hot as hell outside, but the block was lit. One of those days when the whole hood was out, just having a good time for no reason.

I was chilling with a few of the guys when that burnt-orange Lexus pulled up in front of the cookie spot. We all knew that car. Everybody wanted one like it, but only one dude had it—Ricky.

Some Dominican cat from Harlem. Came through here getting money, pulling all the women. A real Rico Suave type. And your mama? She loved that man to death. Worshipped the ground he walked on. He'd say 'jump,' and she'd say 'how high?' He could do no wrong in her eyes.

But that day." Aziz shook his head, laughing. "That day was too funny. Ricky had another chick in the car with him. I don't know who tipped Dee Dee off, but not even five minutes later, here she came—speed walking down the street, hair tied up, shoes laced tight."

Vaughn let out a short laugh.

"Yeah, I heard plenty stories of my moms kickin' ass. I know you ain't lying."

Aziz smirked. "If I'm lyin', I'm flyin', ocki. Your mom's turned that girl every way but loose. But the craziest part? After she whooped that girl's ass, Dee Dee jumped in the passenger seat of Ricky's Lexus—and they drove off like nothing happened."

Vaughn shook his head. "She must've really loved that sucka. Where he at now?"

Aziz shrugged. "Probably dead or in jail, the way he was moving. He was knee-deep in the game."

Before Vaughn could respond, a woman approached their table. It was Astoria.
"Hey, Aziz," she greeted him, completely ignoring Vaughn.

Aziz tilted his glasses down. "Hey, baby girl. How you doing?" He stood and gave her a friendly hug.

"I'm good. Just stopping by. Actually, I wanted to talk to Vaughn," she said, cutting her eyes at him.

"Go ahead, sweetheart, I'm out y'all way. Can I get you a drink?" Aziz offered. "No, thank you, I'm fine," she replied.

"Alright. Tell your mama I said hello," Aziz said before strolling toward the bar. Astoria slid into the booth next to Vaughn.

"Hi, Vaughn," she said softly. The last time they spoke, things got heated. The elephant in the room had to be addressed.

"What's up," he responded dryly.

"Come on, Vaughn, don't act like that toward me." She folded her arms, pouting. He didn't flinch. His eyes stayed glued to the screen.
"I know I said some things I shouldn't have, and I'm sorry, okay?"

"You was doing too much, though, ma. I had enough problems already, and all you did was add to it. I don't need that. I'm sorry," Vaughn said.

"You're right, and I'm sorry. You just really hurt my feelings, Vaughn. You know there's nothing I wouldn't do for you. And you just threw me to the curb for that hoe. That hurt me."

He knew she wasn't lying. He had done her dirty. Astoria had been obsessed with him, but once he fell for Psalm, he cut her off to do right by his girl. He knew it hurt her, which was why he tried to have some empathy.

He turned away from the screen.

"Thank you for the apology, dear. I'm sorry for hurting your feelings. Promise it wasn't my intention. We good?"

Her face lit up. Instead of shaking his hand, she lunged at him, wrapping him in a tight hug.

"Of course we good, Daddy," she laughed, running her hands up his thigh. Her manicured fingers slipped inside his Gucci shorts.

"You should let me show you how sorry I really am, Papa," she whispered seductively. "You know nobody does it like me."

She wasn't lying. Astoria could suck a nail out of a casket.

For a moment, he considered it.

But then Psalm's face flashed in his mind.

As bad as he wanted to let Astoria blow his socks off, his heart wouldn't let him.

"Maybe another time, beloved," he said, gently removing her hand. What he needed to do was find Psalm. His real love.

Astoria rolled her eyes but smirked. "Whatever. I was leaving anyway." "Yeah me too."

As they stood, Aziz called out. "Hey, before you go, Vaughn—your main man Blizz came through the other day."

Vaughn's stomach tightened.

"Oh yeah?" he asked, playing it cool.

Aziz smirked. "You know exactly what he was talking about. Y'all boys need to stop this foolishness."

Vaughn looked away. "Man, you gotta tell him that. Blizz been trippin'."

Aziz shook his head. "Get your life together, youngblood. Before it's too late." Vaughn heard the words but wasn't sure he was ready to listen.

"Nah, for real, man. Y'all two are better than this, and you know it," Aziz said, his voice firm but laced with concern. "You two are practically brothers. You need to make amends, youngblood. And I mean that."

Vaughn looked everywhere but into Aziz's eyes, his pride refusing to let him fold. "Man, you gotta tell him that. But Blizz been trippin', Aziz, I'm telling you. He ain't been himself."

Aziz sighed, removing his glasses and wiping his forehead. "I'ma tell you something real." He leaned forward, lowering his voice. "I've been around the block for a while. I see what's going on. Y'all out here chasing that fast money, living that fast life. Pushing poison. Putting that shit in your bodies. Doing all kinds of wrong. Your minds ain't right."

He paused, looking between Vaughn and Astoria with a weight in his eyes that made them both uneasy.

"You boys are caught up. Caught up in this lifestyle. You're letting Satan trick you with these meaningless luxuries— diamond chains, fancy cars, designer clothes. A green piece of paper." His voice rose, veins popping in his neck. "It ain't about that!"

Aziz was always dropping knowledge, always trying to steer people right. So this wasn't new, but tonight, it hit different.

"It's about making things right with Allah before you leave this earth. Before the day comes when you'll be judged for what you've done. Don't get caught up in this temporary life and its worldly desires." He shook his head, his voice thick with emotion. "Fuck them cars and jewels, ocki. You still got time.

207

Alhamdulilah, you still got a chance to repent, to pray for forgiveness. You too, young sister. I know you ain't no angel either. But Allah is the Most Forgiving, the Most Merciful. Enjoin what's good. Forbid what's evil. Get your life together—please."

He held their gazes, his words settling like stones in their chests.

Vaughn and Astoria nodded, the weight of his message sinking in.

"Appreciate that, Unk," Vaughn said.

"Thank you, Mr. Aziz," Astoria added.

"Nah, for real, man. I love all you youngins. Call Blizz. Y'all squash that shit," Aziz urged.

"Aight, Unk," Vaughn said, trying to wrap things up.

Aziz wasn't done, though. "Keep the brotherhood, man. Because the Prophet Muhammad, peace and blessings be upon him, once said—"

"Aight, Brother Aziz, we gotta go. I'll see you next time, Unk," Vaughn cut in, heading for the door with Astoria before Aziz could start another lecture.

"Inshallah, brother. Take care of y'all selves," Aziz called after them as the door shut behind them.

Vaughn stepped outside, his thoughts racing. I hear you, Unk. But it's real smoke in the streets right now. Ain't got time for all that. He thought to himself.

Mugz emerged from the driver's seat of the parked car, ready to assist, but Vaughn waved him off. "I'm good."

Astoria stood in front of him, tilting her head flirtatiously. "So, you said 'maybe next time.' That mean I should be expecting to see you soon?"

"Yeah, most definitely, baby," Vaughn lied.

She gave him a straight look. "You don't even have my new number. How you plan on seeing me?"

Vaughn pulled out his phone. "What's your number?"

She smirked, snatching his phone and putting her number in, making sure to call herself so she'd have his, too. She wasn't about to let him get away that easy. As she handed the phone back, her expression shifted. "I know you only actin' like this 'cause of that rat-ass bitch you stay up under."

Vaughn shook his head, exhaling. He went in for a hug so he could dip, but Astoria wasn't done.

"I got something to show you," she said, voice low, teasing. "Mhm. I got some shit that's gonna show you exactly how your 'main bitch' really get down. It's in my phone. Yup, right here."

That got Vaughn's attention. His whole demeanor shifted.

"The fuck is you talking about?" he asked, stepping closer.

"Walk me to my car, and I'll show you."

They stood outside the driver's door as she maneuvered to the video on her phone of Tec and Psalm. Just as she was about to hit play—BOOM!

The first shot ripped through the air, snapping Astoria's head back.

A second later, blood splattered across the windshield.

Vaughn barely had time to react.

Gunfire rained down, tearing through the car, glass shattering, metal crunching.

"Get down!" Vaughn yelled, ducking low.

As fast as it came, the car sped off, tires screeching.

His ears were ringing. His adrenaline spiked.

He bolted around the car.

Astoria was slumped.

Her phone lay in her lap, screen still lit, thumb frozen just inches from pressing play. Whatever she was about to show him— he would never see it.

"Fuck," Vaughn muttered, heart pounding.

Mugz ran up. "I know that was your people, boss, but we gotta go. Now."

Vaughn clenched his jaw, eyes lingering on Astoria's lifeless body for one last second.

Then he jumped in the car.

They sped off.

Kuzma the Russian had just sent him another message.

CHAPTER 23: A MOTHER'S BETRAYAL

Vaughn, Mugz, Tec, and Milli sat at a table inside Sylvia's Restaurant on Malcolm X Blvd in Manhattan. The aroma of fried chicken and collard greens filled the air as they waited for their food. Vaughn leaned forward, locking eyes with Tec and Milli.

"I appreciate y'all taking the time to meet with me, so I'm gonna cut straight to the point," he said, his voice low but firm. "You two are my top dogs, so it's only right you expand. We all want more—more money, more cars, more success. I get it. But this war with the Russians is getting out of hand. they just killed Astoria. War is expensive, and I'm not about to keep paying the price. We need to end this."

Tec leaned in, resting his elbows on the table. "You right. So how we supposed to end this shit?" Vaughn smirked. "We kill the head, and the body will fall."
Tec chuckled, shaking his head. "Yeah, I know that much. But how the fuck we supposed to get next to Kuzma? That motherfucker move like the president."

It was true. Taking out Kuzma was damn near a suicide mission.

"Anybody can get touched, my brother. Even the president himself," Vaughn replied coolly. "We catch him while he's vulnerable. I got word that one of the Russians we killed on the bridge—the one in that truck—was Kuzma's favorite nephew. Like a son to him. The funeral service is tomorrow. Kuzma will be there. Security will be tight, so we won't hit him there. But the burial? That's when he'll be most exposed. That's when you move in."

Tec raised an eyebrow. "Hold up. You said 'you guys'—as in we? You ain't getting your hands dirty with this one?"

"Nah," Vaughn said, shaking his head. "That's why I called y'all. You take out Kuzma, and that means we take over his territory. The whole of Brooklyn will be yours and Milli's. And trust me, I'll supply y'all with so much snow they gon' think it's winter year-round."

Tec's mind started racing. This was the opportunity he'd been waiting for. It was about time Vaughn stopped treating him like a little niggas. If he could get Vaughn to front him enough bricks, he'd be set. Then, when the time was right, he'd knock Vaughn off and take everything for himself—including his girl. Sometimes murder was a game of patience, and Tec knew how to play it.

Milli, on the other hand, was focused on the job. He wasn't thinking about power or betrayal—just how they were going to kill Kuzma. Either way, he felt like a walking ghost, and the thought of taking Kuzma out made him grin.

Both brothers extended their hands to Vaughn simultaneously. Vaughn smirked and shook both, sealing the deal.

"Tomorrow," he reminded them.

With that, Vaughn and Mugz rose from their seats and headed for the door. Outside, they climbed into Vaughn's new GLE 63 Benz. Mugz started the engine and pulled into traffic.

After a few minutes of silence, Mugz spoke up. "Yo, boss. You know I don't say much, but that motherfucker Tec don't rub you the wrong way? It's this look he be having on his face when he around you. He try to hide it, but he can't."

Vaughn let out a dry laugh, lighting a fat Backwood filled with exotic Gushers. "Yeah, I noticed. I'd hate to have to put that nigga down. Only 'cause Milli would never forgive me. And I love Milli with all my heart—that's a loyal motherfucker. He don't say much, but his actions speak for him, you feel me? You don't come across too many real ones like that no more."

"That's a fact," Mugz agreed.

Suddenly, red and blue lights lit up the rearview mirror. "Fuck," Gruff muttered. "We got company."
The siren blared, signaling them to pull over. Mugz did so calmly, his hands glued to the steering wheel. Two officers approached the passenger side. As Vaughn rolled down the window, a thick cloud of weed smoke escaped into the night air.

"Get the fuck out of the car!" Detective Grayson barked.

Vaughn smirked. "Can I help you, officer?" he asked arrogantly.

That was all it took.

Detective Grayson yanked the door open, grabbed Vaughn by the arms, and slammed him onto the pavement. The concrete burned his skin as Grayson drove a knee into the back of his head, pressing his face against the ground.

"Yeah, talk that shit now, bitch," the detective sneered.

"Fucking cuff him!" he yelled at his partner, Detective Vega.

They hauled Vaughn to his feet and dragged him toward the black Suburban.

"What happened to Astoria Whitaker?" Detective Vega asked as she patted him down. "Bitch, I don't know," Vaughn spat.

She grabbed the back of his head and slammed it into the side of the car. "Your momma's a bitch," she snapped.

Grayson intervened, stepping between them. "We're taking you to the station. We'll see how much you don't know since you were the last one seen with her."

Vaughn sucked his teeth. "Y'all pussies do whatever the fuck y'all gotta do." "Shut the fuck up," Vega snapped, shoving him into the backseat.

The doors slammed shut. The engine roared to life. They were on their way to the station.

***

Jewel sat in her room upstairs, eating a bowl of Cap'n Crunch while watching her favorite cartoon. She giggled as if she had never seen the episode before. For once, she felt like a child.

She loved that she and Vaughn had a new house—just the two of them. She felt safe with her big brother. Back when she lived with her mother, that feeling was foreign. She loved Dee Dee, but life with her was unpredictable.

Since as far back as she could remember, she had been exposed to things a child shouldn't see—drugs, alcohol, sex, and violence. Having a mother who was a crackhead was disturbing. Jewel used to wake up to the stench of crack smoke before the smell of pancakes and eggs.

And when Dee Dee couldn't get high, she would take her anger out on Jewel for no reason.

That was why she was happy now. She was at peace with the one person who truly protected her.

She was home alone. Vaughn and Gruff had just left when the doorbell suddenly rang. She froze.
Her stomach tightened.

She hadn't been expecting anyone.

Quickly, she shut off the TV and ran to the closet to hide.

Bang! Bang! Bang! Bang!

The knocking grew louder, sending a wave of panic through her little body. Maybe she should run and grab the house phone, call Vaughn—

No! She quickly changed her mind.

Just stay quiet. They'll go away.

Then she heard a voice.

"Jewel! Jewel! It's me! It's your mother. Open the door, girl!"

Her breath caught in her throat.

It was Dee Dee.

She hadn't seen her mother in months—not since the night she almost let Roy molest her. Jewel never looked at her the same after that. She still loved Dee Dee, but trust? That was gone.

Dee Dee banged harder. "I know you're in there! Hurry up and open this door! C'mon, I gotta pee!"

Jewel hesitated. Vaughn had told her not to open the door for anyone. But fear crept in. She remembered the beatings Dee Dee used to give her when she didn't listen. Her hands trembled as she reached for the lock.

"I'm coming," she called out, just so her mother would stop banging like the police. She opened the door—and froze. Dee Dee looked horrible.

This was the worst she had ever seen her. Her arms were streaked with marks Jewel had never noticed before. A wave of stench hit her, making her gag—Dee Dee smelled like she hadn't bathed in weeks.

The life in her once-pretty face was gone. Her eyes and cheeks were sunken in, making her look like a skeleton.

Dee Dee smiled at her, revealing a mouth missing most of its teeth.

"Hey, my baby," she cooed, kneeling down to hug Jewel like nothing had happened between them. Jewel had to hold her breath to keep from gagging.

"You're getting big, girl. You need to stop growing on me!" Dee Dee shook her by the shoulders playfully, but Jewel only stared, uncomfortable.

Dee Dee's eyes wandered past her into the house. "Your brother sure knows how to show off," she muttered. "This is a nice place. I'm mad I didn't get a housewarming invitation." She laughed to herself.

Then she got serious.

"Anyway, come on, let's go. I just talked to Devaughn—he told me to come get you so we can all go to Coney Island like we used to. It's time for us to be a family again."

Jewel's face lit up. Coney Island?
She hadn't been there in forever. It was one of the few happy memories she had with her mother.

"Coney Island?! Oh my gosh! Hold on, let me get my shoes!" she squealed, rushing to put them on.

She tied her laces tight and grabbed her jacket. "Ready!"

But when she looked at Dee Dee, something about her expression made her uneasy.

Her mother was staring at her in a way she had never seen before. A look Jewel couldn't explain, but it made her stomach twist.

Dee Dee forced a smile, trying to mask whatever was running through her mind. "Okay, let's go," she said, turning on her heels and unlocking her car with a beep.

But Jewel hesitated.

Something didn't feel right.

"I thought you said you had to use the bathroom?" she asked.

Dee Dee blinked, as if caught off guard. She glanced up at the sky, thinking of a quick response.

"Shit, it went away. You had me standing outside banging on the door forever. Forget about that. Come on."

Her tone was different now. Annoyed. Rushed.

Jewel's gut screamed at her.

"Umm… I don't wanna go anymore. I'll just wait for Vaughn to get back." Dee Dee's entire face changed.

"You got two seconds to get your ass in that car. I'm not playing with you." Jewel turned to slam the door and make a run for it—
But Dee Dee was faster.

She caught the door just before it shut, shoving her way inside. Before Jewel could reach the stairs, Dee Dee grabbed a fistful of her hair, yanking her backward.

Jewel screamed.

A silver blade appeared in Dee Dee's hand. She pressed it to her daughter's neck.

"Alright, playtime is over, you little bitch. Get your raggedy ass in the car before I nut the fuck up on you."

Jewel sobbed.

"Shut that crying up. I don't give a fuck about none of that," Dee Dee hissed, dragging her outside. "Got me running around chasing after your lil' ass."

She threw Jewel into the car, slammed the door shut, and sped off. Dee Dee didn't care that she had just kidnapped her own daughter.

CHAPTER 24: THE FUNERAL HIT

The burial site was packed with mourners, heads bowed under a sea of black coats. Heavy rain poured from the gray sky, drumming against the cherrywood casket. The imam's voice rose over the storm, steady and unwavering, delivering prayers for the dead.

But grief wasn't the only thing in the air—it was thick with tension, a silent undercurrent of vengeance and unfinished business.

Kuzma stood at the edge of the open grave, his men forming a protective circle around him. His face was stone, but his eyes burned with grief and fury. As his nephew was lowered into the ground, he scanned the crowd, knowing better than to drop his guard.

Especially here.

From a hill overlooking the cemetery, Tec lay camouflaged among the dense brush, his rifle resting on a boulder. The scope was fixed on Kuzma. He pressed a finger to his earpiece, his voice low but firm.

"Alright, twin. Move swift. In and out. Make it count—you already know what the fuck going on."

Milli adjusted the hood draped over his head, blending seamlessly into the sea of mourners. In his hands, he clutched a bouquet of cheap flowers, his posture hunched, his presence unassuming. Tec could've taken the shot from his position, but hitting a moving target from 200 meters without drawing immediate attention required a level of precision even he wasn't willing to gamble on.

This had to be close and personal.

Milli kept moving, his eyes locked on Kuzma as he stepped closer to the grave. The weight of the blade pressed against his sleeve, its cool metal a silent reminder of what needed to be done.

"Stay sharp," Tec whispered through the earpiece. Through the scope, he tracked Kuzma's every move. "You got ten seconds before his men close the circle."

Milli took another step forward, brushing against a mourner. No one noticed. The grief in the air made them blind, oblivious to the predator in their midst.

Then came the moment.

Kuzma shifted slightly, his guard down just enough.

Milli struck.

His hand shot out, the blade gliding between Kuzma's ribs with a swift, practiced motion.

Kuzma stiffened, his breath hitching as pain overtook him. Milli stepped in, pulling him close in what looked like a comforting embrace.

To anyone watching, it was just one mourner consoling another. But this was the hug of death.
Tec grinned from his position. "It's done."

Kuzma's body trembled. His knees buckled slightly, but he remained standing, his weight masking the fatal wound. Milli tightened his grip for a moment before letting go, slipping back into the crowd like a shadow fading into the night.

Kuzma's men were too slow.

"Boss?" one of them called, eyes darting to their leader's pale face. Alarm rippled through them as they noticed the blood spreading beneath his coat.

But by the time they realized what had happened, Milli was already gone, disappearing past the cemetery gates, the bloody weapon discarded at his feet.

Tec exhaled. The job was done.

But as he watched Kuzma sway on his feet, an urge crept up on him, something dark and irresistible.

His finger hovered over the trigger.

"Fuck it. It's worth the try."

He pulled it.

The gunshot cut through the rain like a whip. The bullet tore through Kuzma's chest. His body jerked violently as the impact knocked him off balance—his final fall landing him directly onto the casket below.

Two bodies. One grave.

For a split second, the world stood still. Then—chaos. Screams erupted. Mourners ducked for cover, scattering like startled birds. Kuzma's men barked orders, drawing their weapons, searching for the unseen shooter.

But Tec and Milli were already gone. Mission complete.

***

The room was ice cold, but sweat beaded along Vaughn's temple as he leaned back in the hard metal chair. His wrists rested on the edge of the table, fingers tapping the surface—slow and steady. It was the only sound in the room besides the faint hum of the air conditioning.

He wasn't new to this.

But this time felt different.

The weight in his chest pressed harder than usual.

The door swung open, and in walked Detective Grayson, smirking like he already knew how this was going to play out. In one hand, he carried a folder; in the other, a Styrofoam cup of coffee. The door slammed shut behind him, the sound bouncing off the cinder block walls.

"You look comfortable, Vaughn." Grayson dropped into the chair across from him, setting the folder on the table. "Glad to see you're making yourself at home. Might as well get used to it—you're gonna be here for a while."

Vaughn tilted his head slightly, offering a half-smile. "I ain't got shit to say, so you might as well save your breath, nigga."

Grayson chuckled, leaning forward. "Oh, you'll talk. They always do. Let me show you why."

He flipped open the folder and pulled out a series of photographs. Then, a brown paper evidence bag. Inside was a phone—bagged and tagged. He slid it across the table toward Vaughn.

"You recognize this?" Grayson asked. "That's Astoria's phone. Found it at the scene of her murder. And what's interesting is—she called you less than a minute before she died." He paused, letting the words sink in. "That's not a good look."

Vaughn's jaw tightened, but he said nothing.

Grayson continued, pulling out more photos. "And here's the best part. Your little friend Astoria? She was helping us out. Gave us some good tips. Told us about Sada riding dirty with a trunk full of product. She was feeding us real intel." He took a slow sip of his coffee before adding, "I wouldn't be telling you this if she was still breathing."

Vaughn leaned back, crossing his arms. "You don't know shit." Grayson smirked and slid another photo across the table. This time, it wasn't Astoria or a crime scene.

It was Blizz's mugshot.

"Well, let me tell you what I do know," Grayson said, tapping the picture. "Blizz has a warrant out for Ronnie's murder. Hair fibers found in the car. DNA evidence. He's done."

Grayson leaned in, voice dropping to a whisper.

"And you? You're next."

Vaughn's stomach twisted, but he kept his expression blank.

"We've got a mountain of evidence piling up," Grayson continued. "And the feds? They're picking up the case. You know what that means, don't you? Federal charges. No parole. Mandatory minimums. You'll be sitting in a cell for the rest of your life—if Omega doesn't put a bullet in your head first."

At the mention of Omega, Vaughn's façade cracked—just for a second. A slight twitch in his jaw.

Grayson caught it immediately.

"Ah, there it is," the detective said, grinning. "You know as well as I do—Omega doesn't give a damn about you. You're a pawn. Expendable. So why the fuck are you protecting him? You think he'll do the same for you?"

Vaughn stared at the table, his mind racing.

He knew Omega wouldn't protect him. Not if it came down to it. Omega was always three steps ahead, always cutting off loose ends before they became a liability.

He'd seen what happened to those who got in the way— loyalty meant nothing in this game.

Grayson leaned even closer, voice barely above a whisper. "Here's the deal, Vaughn. Give us Omega. Tell us what we need to know, and maybe—just maybe—we can cut you a deal. Keep you out of federal hands. Keep you breathing."

Vaughn swallowed hard. His heart pounded, but his voice stayed cold. "Nigga, eat a dick. I don't snitch."
Grayson nodded slowly, almost sympathetically. "Loyalty's cute, but it won't keep you out of a casket."

He paused, letting the words settle.

"Blizz is done. You're next. And once Omega knows we're circling him, you're a dead man walking."

The words hung heavy in the air. Vaughn knew the game.

He knew cops would say anything to make you fold, to break you down until you gave them what they wanted. But he wasn't going for that.

He sat back, waiting for Grayson to run out of bullshit and tell him he could go. Grayson sighed, tapping the table lightly. "Alright. I see how this is gonna go."
He stood up, heading for the door, then stopped.

"Oh, I almost forgot."

He pulled out Astoria's phone and set it on the table. The screen lit up with a video. "When we got to the scene, this was still playing."

Vaughn's stomach dropped as the image filled the screen. Psalm. And Tec.

The video showed her standing outside a door, leaning in close. Then she stretched up on her tiptoes and wrapped her arms around Tec's neck. His hands slid down her back, gripping her ass.

Vaughn's fists clenched under the table.

"Damn," Grayson said, shaking his head in mock sympathy. "That's your homie, right? Your right-hand man?"

He let the words settle, pushing the dagger deeper into Vaughn's heart.

It felt like someone had hit him in the stomach with a pillowcase full of bricks. A wave of hurt, anger, and betrayal overtook him.

"I see your type all the time, Vaughn," Grayson continued, voice calm. "And every time, it's guys like you who finish last.

There's no loyalty in this game. You're trying to protect people who don't give two shits about you."

Vaughn's mind raced.

This wasn't about loyalty anymore.

It was about survival.

And from the looks of it, everyone was out for themselves.

Grayson pressed on, his tone shifting to something almost fatherly. "Everyone's gonna turn on you, man. You still wanna play the tough guy? Give us what we need, and make it easier on yourself."

Vaughn locked eyes with him, his voice low and sharp.

"Give you what you need?" He let out a humorless chuckle. "Nigga, I wouldn't spit on you if you was on fire."

Grayson raised an eyebrow, then smirked. "Alright. Tough guy."

He pushed the chair back and let the door slam shut behind him, leaving Vaughn alone with nothing but his thoughts.

And right now, those thoughts were dangerous.

CHAPTER 25: BLOOD RUNS DEEPER

Detective Vega stepped into the dimly lit warehouse, the sharp echo of her YSL heels cutting through the silence. Dressed casually, off-duty, but still carrying her badge and gun on her hip, she exuded both confidence and authority. She leaned against an old wooden desk, slipping off her Dolce & Gabbana shades, her gaze locking onto Omega.

He sat on a worn-out leather couch, a cigar smoldering between his fingers, his expression unreadable. He studied her with mild curiosity, waiting for an explanation.

Vega reached into the plush mink jacket draped over her shoulders and pulled out a thick manila envelope. She tossed it onto the table between them.

"The feds are sniffing around your operation," she said flatly. "They're taking over the case. My hands are tied now."

Omega picked up the folder and skimmed through its contents, his expression darkening. "And what does that mean for us, Vega? You know I don't play well with outsiders."

She crossed her arms. "It means you keep your mouth shut if things get messy. My family's not about to let you screw this up for everyone. They've invested too much."

Omega's eyes flicked up from the folder. He knew what she meant. Her Colombian family had played a major role in his success—without them, he never would've found the type of connect he had now.

He exhaled a thick cloud of smoke. "Your family needs to remember who's keeping their business alive out here. If I go down, your whole empire crumbles."

Vega stepped closer, resting a manicured hand on his shoulder. Her voice softened. "You're too smart to let it come to that, baby. Just... be careful. You've got a lot to lose."

The tension in Omega's shoulders eased slightly. "You're right."

He stood, taking a step toward her—his eyes lingering. Vega had that undeniable pull. Whether she was in uniform or dressed casually, she turned heads everywhere she went. She was stunning, and Omega was in love with her, though she had no idea. He leaned in for a kiss—

The warehouse door creaked open.

Vaughn entered, a duffle bag slung over his shoulder. His eyes widened the second he saw Vega. His body tensed, his hand instinctively reaching for the gun tucked in the small of his back.

"What's she doing here?" he asked, his tone edged with suspicion. Omega waved him off. "Relax. She's cool."

Vaughn wasn't convinced. He moved cautiously toward them, his grip still tight on the strap of the duffle.

"Vaughn, I brought you here because I need you to understand something—Vega is on our team," Omega said, relighting his cigar.

Vaughn scoffed. "Yeah? And how the fuck am I supposed to trust this bitch?"

Vega's expression darkened as she stepped toward him. "Watch your mouth, puta. You can trust that I'm the reason your sorry ass isn't sitting on Rikers Island fighting indictments."

Vaughn clenched his jaw, but before he could respond, Omega interjected. "She's been working with us for a while. She's the only reason we're not locked up already. She's been keeping us two steps ahead of Grayson."

The mention of Detective Grayson made Vaughn's eyes narrow. The cop had been relentless, treating his job like a personal vendetta.

Vega sighed, adjusting the envelope under her arm. "But Grayson's not the problem anymore. The alphabet boys are snooping around. You two need to figure out your next move. I'll do what I can on my end, but don't expect much."

"I'll handle it," Omega assured her.

She held out her hand. "Good. Now take care of me so I can be on my way." Omega gestured to Vaughn. "Give her the bag."

Vaughn hesitated for a moment before tossing the duffle onto the table. "That's half a mil in there."

Vega smirked as she picked it up. "It better be."

Without another word, she turned on her heels and disappeared through the warehouse doors, the heavy creak echoing behind her.

Vaughn turned to Omega, his face twisted in confusion. "Yo, what's the deal with her? Since when you got cops in your pocket?"

Omega exhaled, putting out his cigar in the ashtray. "Don't worry about Vega. She's got her own reasons for being here."

"Man, you better watch her. Cops ain't loyal to nobody but themselves," Vaughn warned.

Omega chuckled, shaking his head. "You still got a lot to learn, kid. She ain't just any cop. She's family business."

Vaughn nodded slowly, letting the words sink in. But something still didn't sit right with him. "All this fed shit she's talking about… I hope it ain't shaking you up, old man."

Omega shot him a sharp look but didn't respond right away. He leaned back against the desk, his face unreadable.

"I've been through worse storms than this. You wouldn't understand." "Try me," Vaughn challenged.
Omega paused, then smirked faintly. "You remind me of someone I used to know. Same fire. Same attitude."

"Yeah? Who's that?"

Omega's smirk faded. "Just someone who learned the hard way that blood runs deeper than loyalty."

Vaughn narrowed his eyes. "What's that supposed to mean?"

Omega shrugged, abruptly changing the subject. "It means you need to focus. Handle your business, and maybe one day, you'll see the bigger picture."

Before Vaughn could press further, his phone buzzed in his pocket. He pulled it out and saw Mugz's name flashing across the screen.

"Yo," Vaughn answered.

Mugz's voice came through, tense and panicked. "Boss, we got a big problem." Vaughn's stomach dropped. "What?"

There was a pause, then Mugz said something that made his blood run cold. "It's Jewel. Somebody's taken her.

***

Blizz trudged through the alley, the cold New York wind biting at his face. His hoodie was pulled low, but it did nothing to stop the sweat trickling down his temples. He could feel the eyes on him—watchful, suspicious. The whispers at the corner store, the way conversations stopped when he walked by. It was all too obvious now.

He was a wanted man.

Leaning against a brick wall, he tried to steady his breath. A poster flapped beside him, partially torn, but the words burned into his mind.

WANTED: TERELL SHARPE AKA BLIZZ – ARMED AND DANGEROUS. SUSPECT IN THE MURDER OF RONNIE JOHNSON.

His name. His face. But no mention of Vaughn.

His fingers clenched into fists. We both pulled that trigger. So why the fuck am I the only one being hunted? The thought clawed at his mind, bitter and relentless. Did Vaughn set me up? He'd been robbing their own spots—was this payback?

A shadow moved at the alley's entrance. Blizz tensed, heart pounding as his hand gripped the Glock 45 in his waistband. He exhaled slowly, waiting. Then the figure stepped into the dim light.

Vaughn.

Their eyes locked—anger, betrayal, and something deeper lurking beneath. Blizz didn't hesitate. He pulled his gun and leveled it at Vaughn's chest.

"What the fuck you doin' here?" His voice was low, shaking with rage. "You set me up, didn't you, nigga?"

Vaughn didn't flinch. His jaw clenched, but his hands stayed open at his sides. "Blizz, I didn't set you up. I swear on everything." He took a cautious step forward. "I don't know how they pinned it all on you. We both did that job."

Blizz's grip tightened. His finger twitched on the trigger. "Then why the fuck is it just me on every damn poster? Huh? Just me!"

Vaughn hesitated, guilt flickering across his face. "I don't know. But listen, we got bigger problems." His voice cracked. "Jewel's gone. Somebody took her. And Tec—man, Tec's been with Psalm."

The words sliced through Blizz like a blade. His grip loosened on the gun. Jewel—his family. And Psalm? That was supposed to be Vaughn's girl.

Blizz lowered the Glock slightly, his face unreadable. The world around him felt like it was crumbling.

Vaughn stepped closer, desperation in his eyes. "I need your help. The Feds are closing in on Omega. Everything's falling apart."

Blizz stared at him for a long moment. Then, he shook off Vaughn's hand, his voice cold. "Nah. That's your mess to clean up now." He turned, taking a step back. "We were brothers once. But I can't trust you no more."

He walked away, not looking back.

The wind howled through the alley, drowning out Vaughn's voice as he called after him. Each step felt heavier, the weight of betrayal pressing down. Running wouldn't save him.

But staying?

That was a death sentence.

CHAPTER 26: COLLATERAL DAMAGE

Dee Dee's hands trembled on the wheel, her grip slick with sweat. Her eyes flicked to the rearview mirror, where Little Jewel sat in the back seat, wide-eyed and silent. The girl didn't cry, didn't speak—just stared, her tiny fingers clutching the torn sleeve of her mother's jacket.

Streetlights blurred past, casting flickering shadows across Dee Dee's gaunt face. She hadn't slept in days. The craving gnawed at her insides, louder than the whisper of motherly guilt clawing at the back of her mind.

"Don't worry, baby. Mama's got this," she muttered, her voice hollow.

She knew exactly where she was going—a run-down crackhouse in Freeport. The dealers there owed her, but tonight, they were calling in their debt.

When she pulled up, Tec was already there, leaning against the wall, half-hidden in the shadows. A slow smirk curled across his face as he spotted Little Jewel in the back seat. His fingers twitched at his sides, barely concealing his anticipation. This was more than just an exchange—this was leverage.

"You're late, Dee Dee," Tec said, his voice a low growl.

"Just take her and gimme what you promised," she snapped, desperation laced in every word.

Tec's eyes glinted. He reached into the pocket of his Purple designer jeans and pulled out a baggie of brown powder, letting it dangle between his fingers just out of reach. The product was the size of a golf ball—enough to drown her in oblivion for days.

"First things first," he said, nodding toward Jewel. "Hand her over." Dee Dee hesitated.

Jewel whimpered, her tiny hands gripping her mother's sleeve tighter. "Mama, please," she whispered.

For a second, something flickered in Dee Dee's hollowed-out eyes—doubt, hesitation, maybe even guilt. But then, the hunger kicked in, overpowering everything else.

She unclenched her fingers and pushed Jewel forward.

Tec caught the little girl by the shoulder and turned her away without a second glance. Dee Dee snatched the baggie from his hand, already lost in her own world, the high swallowing any second thoughts she might've had.

Tec led Jewel inside the house. The dim overhead light flickered, casting eerie shadows along the crumbling walls. The place smelled of smoke, sweat, and something rotten. Jewel's little body trembled—fear tightening around her small chest.

In the back room, Psalm sat on the edge of a chair, her arms crossed, her face unreadable. When Tec walked in with the child, her eyes flicked over Jewel, unimpressed.

"This is it?" she asked, voice cold.

Tec nodded. "Leverage. Just like you wanted."

Psalm stood and crouched down to Jewel's level, tilting her head as she studied the girl. "Your brother's going to regret everything he did," she whispered.

Jewel's bottom lip quivered, but she didn't make a sound. The game had changed. Vaughn was about to feel pain like never before.

The air outside the abandoned basketball court cut like a blade, sharp and merciless, but it was nothing compared to the fire burning inside Vaughn. The chain nets swayed in the cold wind, the cracked pavement covered in faded gang tags—this place used to be an escape. Now, it was a war room.

His soldiers stood in a tight semicircle, their breath misting in the night air, shifting uneasily as he paced like a caged animal. His fists clenched so hard his knuckles were bone-white, his eyes burning with a rage too deep to hold.

"They took Little Jewel." His voice was raw, venomous. "My little sister. And y'all standing here like this is a damn drill?"

A rusted trash can went flying, crashing against the chain-link fence. The sound barely registered over the storm inside him. He kicked over a wooden bench, the splinters scattering at his feet. His chest heaved. His whole body shook.

"I want every block in Long Island flipped upside down!" His voice cracked with fury. "Knock on doors, smash windows, pull motherfuckers out their beds if you have to! I don't give a damn who gets hurt! If they breathe wrong, put 'em on their knees and ask questions later." His voice dropped to a deadly growl. "You bring me my sister, or I swear to God, I'm catching a body tonight."

No one questioned him. One by one, his soldiers nodded, peeling away into the night like shadows.

But Vaughn wasn't finished. His jaw clenched as he turned. "Cipher."

From the back of the group, Cipher stepped forward. The air around him seemed to still. Tall, lean, with eyes as cold as the steel he carried, Cipher never spoke unless necessary. His name suited him—silent, unreadable, dangerous.

Vaughn walked up until they were inches apart, his breath hot with rage. "I got another job for you."

Cipher barely blinked. "What is it?"

Vaughn's teeth clenched so hard his jaw ached. "You know Tec." Cipher smirked faintly. "Yeah. What about him?"

Vaughn's stomach twisted. The words nearly caught in his throat, but his fury pushed them out. "That snake broke the rules. He has betrayed me so far as to take a shot at Psalm. My girl." His voice turned to gravel. "The same girl who left me 'cause of what I did... what I had to do." His hand shook as he reached into his pocket, pulling out a fat stack of bills. "I want him dead. No second chances. No mistakes."

Cipher took the money, eyes blank. "Consider it done."

Vaughn's hand trembled as Cipher turned away. The weight of everything was crushing him—the betrayal, the rage, the loneliness clawing at his insides. And then—

His phone rang.

The screen lit up with a name that sliced through him like a blade. Psalm.

For a second, everything stopped. The court disappeared. The cold faded. All that existed was her name, glowing in his palm.

His fingers hovered before he finally answered. His voice was rough, almost broken. "Psalm…"

Silence. Heavy, thick. Then, her voice—low, cold, but trembling with something deeper. "You sound surprised to hear from me."

His throat tightened. "What do you want?"

She laughed, but there was no joy in it. Just pain. Just hate. "What do I want? You really don't get it, do you?" Her voice wavered, but she steadied it with venom. "You took everything from me, Vaughn. My uncle. My trust. My heart."

His chest ached. "Psalm, I—"

"Save it!" she snapped, her voice raw with fury. "You think you can just kill Ronnie and everything stays the same? You think I'd let that slide?"

His head dropped. "You think I wanted this? I wake up every day wishing things were different. Wishing I didn't lose you."

A bitter silence. Then, her voice—steady now. Calculated. Ice-cold. "Well, I've got Jewel. She's with me." His blood ran cold.

"If you want her back," she continued, "you're going to give me the one thing I want—Omega. The one who ordered the hit on my uncle."

Vaughn's breath came fast, his mind racing. "You want me to turn in Omega?"

Her voice trembled—anger, pain, something breaking inside her. "Bring him to me. Tomorrow night. 9 PM. You set him up, or you'll never see your sister again."

His grip tightened around the phone. "You're playing a dangerous game, Psalm." She let out a shaky breath. "I've got nothing left to lose."

Then, the line went dead.

Vaughn stood frozen, the weight of it all pressing down on him like a collapsing building. His pulse thundered. His breath came in short bursts.

And then—BOOM!

His fist slammed against the rusted pole, pain jolting up his arm. His eyes were wild, his chest rising and falling like a man drowning in fire.

Tomorrow night.

The clock was ticking.

And if he played this wrong, Jewel's life—and his own— would be lost forever.

CHAPTER 27: BLOOD FOR BLOOD

The narrow alley behind the old garage was soaked in shadows, the damp air thick with oil, mildew, and old secrets. Tec stood in the dim glow of a flickering streetlight, his jaw tight, eyes restless. He reached into his coat, pulling out a thick duffle bag, heavy with weight.

Milli stood in front of him, silent as always, hood pulled low. His brother's stillness had always unnerved people, but Tec understood it. Milli didn't need words. His presence spoke enough.

Tec exhaled sharply and clapped a firm hand on Milli's shoulder. "Listen up, bro. You're gonna take this bag to the apartment in the back of the alley—third floor, last door on the left. You already know the routine. Walk in, drop it off to the workers, and walk out. No extra moves. No extra time." His voice dropped lower. "Make it fast."

Milli gave a slow nod, reaching for the duffle.

Tec hesitated. He studied his brother for a beat, then reached for the thick gold chain hanging from his own neck. He unclasped it, the heavy links cool in his palm. The pendant gleamed under the dim streetlight—a lion's head, its eyes set with tiny diamonds. A signature piece. Everyone knew it.

Wordlessly, Tec stepped forward and fastened it around Milli's neck. The weight of it rested against Milli's chest, solid and unmistakable.

"They need to think you're me," Tec murmured. He exhaled, glancing around as if the walls had ears. "Vaughn's got people watching. Cops, too. If I move wrong, it's over for me. But you?" He looked into his brother's eyes, searching for hesitation and finding none. "You know the routine. Remember twin. In, out, no risks."

Milli's fingers brushed the chain for a second, then he pulled his hood up and slung the duffle over his shoulder. Without another word, he turned and disappeared into the alley, his movements precise, controlled—a mirror of Tec.

Milli's footsteps echoed as he neared the end of the alley. The apartment was a rundown, two-story building with boarded-up windows and a single, flickering porch light. He climbed the fire escape with ease, his every motion sharp and efficient.

Inside, the hallway reeked of old cigarettes and sweat. When he reached the last door, he gave a single knock—Tec's knock. A pause, then the door cracked open.

A wiry man with yellowed teeth and tired eyes peered out. His gaze immediately dropped to the lion-head pendant, and his suspicion faded.

"'Bout time," the man muttered, stepping aside.

Milli said nothing. He walked in, set the duffle down, and turned to leave. The workers barely acknowledged him. To them, he was just Tec doing his usual business.

Smooth. Just like always.

He was back outside in under two minutes.

Cipher waited in the shadows, heart hammering. His grip tightened around his gun as he watched the figure move through the alley. The same height. The same build. The same gold chain.

His pulse quickened. This was it. This was Tec.

Cipher stepped forward, emerging from the darkness, gun raised. His voice was cold, sharp as a blade.

"Tec," he growled. "Time to pay for your sins."

Milli stopped. The dim light from the street reflected off the lion pendant. His face was still obscured by the hood, cigarette smoke curling from his lips.

Cipher sneered. "Explain why you crossed Vaughn. Maybe I'll make it quick." Silence.

Cipher's fingers twitched against the trigger. Something about the way Tec—no, this man—stood there sent an uneasy prickle down his spine. But he shoved the feeling away.

"I said talk, nigga!" His voice cracked with frustration.

Milli took a slow drag from the cigarette, let the smoke drift into the cold air, then flicked it to the ground. The ember flared and died.

And then he moved. Fast. Cipher barely had time to react before Milli was on him, knocking the gun aside with a brutal swing. A shot fired, wild—missing its target.

Milli lunged, driving an elbow into Cipher's ribs. The impact stole Cipher's breath, sent him staggering back, but Milli didn't let up. Another hit—sharp, ruthless—this time to Cipher's jaw. His head snapped to the side, blood spraying against the alley wall.

Cipher cursed, swinging wildly. Milli ducked. Slipped. Moved like a phantom. He hit Cipher again, knuckles cracking against his cheekbone. The force sent Cipher reeling, his back slamming against the brick wall.

For a moment, Cipher's vision blurred. He was losing.

A growl of frustration ripped from Cipher's throat. He reached for the knife in his boot and swung.

The blade caught flesh.

Milli stumbled back, blood darkening his hoodie. But still— no sound. No reaction. Cipher's eyes widened. How the hell was he still standing?

Milli stepped forward, slow and steady, as if the pain was nothing but a whisper. Cipher gritted his teeth. This wasn't normal. He faked left, then lunged again, slashing across Milli's side. Another hit. Another deep wound. Still, Milli didn't flinch.

Fear crept into Cipher's chest. This man was a ghost.

But ghosts could still die.

With a desperate roar, Cipher drove the knife forward— burying it deep into Milli's chest. Milli's body stiffened.

A slow exhale, a shudder.

The fight was over.

Milli swayed for a second before his legs gave out. He collapsed, his body hitting the pavement with a dull thud.

Cipher staggered back, gripping his own ribs, sucking in ragged breaths. His vision blurred. His hands trembled. Blood—his and Milli's—painted the alley floor.

He had won. Barely.

Then—footsteps.

Cipher barely had the strength to lift his head before he saw him. Tec.

Tec's world fractured.

He barely remembered running, barely felt his knees hit the pavement beside Milli. His hands shook as he reached for his twin, the gold lion pendant now dull with blood.

"Milli…" The name came out broken, torn from his throat. He swallowed hard, chest rising and falling in short, sharp gasps.

He wasn't breathing. He wasn't moving.

Cipher coughed, choking on his own blood, his body slumped against the wall. His eyes fluttered open, barely holding on.

Tec's head snapped toward him, his grief twisting into something sharp, something deadly. "Who sent you?" Tec's voice was low, but it carried violence.

Cipher tried to smirk, but all that came out was a pained wheeze.

Tec's hand moved fast. A gun, aimed steady. No hesitation.

Bang.

The shot echoed through the alley. Cipher's body jerked. Then—stillness.

Silence.

Then—buzz.

Tec's eyes flicked down. Cipher's phone vibrated in his pocket.

He reached over, pulled it out, and saw the name flashing across the screen.

Vaughn.

His grip on the phone tightened. He hit answer.

"He's gone," Tec said, his voice void of emotion.

A pause. Then Vaughn's voice, crackling through the speaker.

"Cipher? You did it?"

Tec's jaw clenched. His eyes burned as he looked at his brother's lifeless body. "No," he said, voice sharp as a blade. "You did it. You got my twin killed."

***

The evening air pressed heavy against Vaughn's chest as he leaned back in his leather chair, staring out at the city lights. The streets below pulsed with life, but inside, everything felt hollow. His mind was trapped in a loop, ticking down the minutes to 9 PM—the moment everything would come to a head. He pictured Psalm, standing there with his baby sister Jewel in her grasp, her cold eyes demanding the unthinkable.

The cost of his sister's life? Omega.

Omega—the man who had given him his first shot when he was just another kid trying to claw his way out of nothing. His mentor, his supplier, maybe even something more. Turning on him wasn't just betrayal—it was suicide. But if he didn't, he'd never see Jewel again.

"Damn," Vaughn muttered, rubbing his temples.

Mugz deep voice cut through his thoughts. "You can't give her Omega, man. You do that, you're done. No product, no protection. Omega's got your back, even if he don't show it."

Vaughn clenched his jaw. "I know. But if I don't give her Omega, I lose Jewel. I can't let that happen."

Mugz folded his massive arms, his presence filling the room like a human wall. "Then we need a way to flip this. Make sure Omega walks away, Psalm gets what she came for, and you get your sister back."

Vaughn stared at the dim-lit ceiling, his mind working through the impossible. There was only one person who could make this work. A long shot, but better than nothing.

He grabbed his phone and dialed.

The line clicked. "Detective Vega."

"It's Vaughn. I got something for you."

There was a pause. Then her voice sharpened. "What kind of something?" "Omega's in danger. He's gonna be at the old rail yard tonight at 9 PM."

Another pause. "Why are you telling me this?" Suspicion laced her words, but beneath it, curiosity.

"Because he trusts you. And… I know you care about him." Vaughn hesitated, his voice lowering. "You're the only one who can keep him safe."

Detective Vega's sigh crackled through the line. "I'll be there. Don't make me regret this, Vaughn."

"You won't."

He hung up, exhaling slowly. The first piece was in place. Now came the next move.

He dialed again. The phone rang twice before a familiar gravelly voice answered. "Vaughn. Been a minute."
"Yeah. We need to talk. Tonight. 9 PM. Old rail yard. Just you and me."

Omega went silent for a beat. "Funny. I was gonna call you. Got something to tell you. Something you need to know about…"

Vaughn felt his gut tighten. "Then I guess we'll see each other there."

He ended the call and stared out at the city. The plan was risky—built on fractured trust, manipulation, and the thin hope that it wouldn't all collapse around him. But if it worked, Omega would walk away, Psalm would get her revenge, and Jewel would come home.

All he had to do now… was pray everything went right.

CHAPTER 28: A SHOT AT REDEMPTION

The bar was dim, worn down by the weight of the stories it had absorbed over the years. The low hum of a TV in the corner blended with the occasional clink of glass against wood. The scent of aged whiskey and stale smoke lingered in the air like ghosts of past confessions.

Blizz sat at the far end of the counter, shoulders hunched, eyes hollow. His fingers toyed with the smooth surface of a Percocet pill before he tossed it back, chasing it with a long swig of Patrón. The burn in his throat did little to wash away the ache in his chest.

Behind the bar, Aziz wiped a glass clean with slow, deliberate strokes. His quiet demeanor masked the concern lining his face. He had watched Blizz grow up, seen the hunger in his eyes as a kid, the weight on his shoulders as a man. And tonight, he saw something else—something dangerous.

"You good, Blizz?" Aziz's voice was steady, but there was a softness beneath it. Blizz didn't lift his head. "Good enough."

Aziz set the glass down, folding his arms across his chest. His brows knitted together as he studied the younger man. "You don't look good, son. What's going on with you and Vaughn?"

Blizz exhaled sharply, shaking his head. Vaughn was the last thing on his mind. He was a wanted man with nowhere to run. But the bitterness still sat heavy on his tongue.

"Ain't no 'me and Vaughn' no more," he muttered. "He let that money change him. Forgot where we came from. Forgot who put in the work when he couldn't handle the weight. Thought I wasn't good enough to run things." A bitter laugh escaped him. "I was there from day one. Now he acts like I don't even matter."

Aziz sighed, his eyes heavy with understanding. "This life can twist a man, make him forget. But holding onto that hurt... it only eats at you, Blizz."

Blizz looked away, his gaze unfocused. "It already has."

Aziz hesitated for a moment before speaking carefully. "I heard about Jewel. Two detectives, Grayson and Vega, were here earlier. They got a call. Sounded like Vaughn found out where she is. Might be something going down tonight."

Blizz's fingers curled around his glass. "He asked me for help." He shook his head. "Told him to go to hell. I don't want nothing to do with him."

Aziz leaned in, his voice low and urgent. "Blizz, you've been carrying this burden too long. Maybe it's time to let go."

Blizz stared into his drink, the weight of his choices pressing against his ribs. "Can't. My hands are too dirty."

Aziz's gaze softened. "Son, no hand is too dirty for God's mercy. Allah forgives all sins. You're not beyond saving. No one is."

Blizz's throat tightened. Blood spilled. Trust broken. The choices that led him here. A tear slid down his cheek, warm and uncontrollable. "Don't know if I can change."

Aziz placed a firm yet gentle hand on his shoulder. "You can. Allah loves those who turn back to Him. It's never too late."

Blizz swallowed hard, his voice barely above a whisper. "I don't deserve that kind of forgiveness."

Aziz's voice grew firmer. "You think any of us do? Forgiveness isn't earned, Blizz. It's given. You just have to ask for it."

For the first time in years, Blizz wanted peace.

Aziz's voice was calm, steady. "Take the shahada, Blizz. Bear witness. Let God wash away what's behind you."

Blizz's lips trembled. He nodded, his voice cracking. "I... I want to."

Aziz smiled gently. "Repeat after me."

Blizz closed his eyes, tears streaming as he whispered the words.

"Ash-hadu an la ilaha illa Allah, wa ash-hadu anna Muhammadan rasul Allah."

The words trembled on his lips, each syllable pulling him away from the abyss. When he finished, a shiver ran through him—like a weight lifting, like chains breaking. Relief, pure and cleansing, flooded his body.

Aziz squeezed his shoulder. "You're free now, Blizz. A new life. A new path." Blizz wiped his face, his voice shaky. "Thank you."

Aziz nodded. "I'm closing down the bar. Moving to Atlanta. Fresh start for me too. Maybe it's time for you to find yours."

Blizz looked at him, the corners of his mouth twitching into the faintest smile. "Maybe I will." Aziz smiled back. "May Allah bless your path, Blizz."

Too Late 2 Apologize: Paid in Pain

As Blizz stood to leave, for the first time in years, he felt a sliver of hope—a promise that the darkness didn't have to win.

CHAPTER 29: BLOOD IN THE WATER

The air was thick with salt and gasoline, the rhythmic slosh of water against the rotting pier filling the silence. An old industrial dock sprawled into the black ocean, its rusted bones jutting out like a graveyard of forgotten deals. The distant city lights barely reached this far, leaving everything cloaked in shadow and uncertainty.

From the cover of a derelict warehouse, Detective Vega watched through narrowed eyes. Beside her, Detective Grayson leaned casually against a rusted shipping container, a cigarette dangling between his fingers.

"We should move in before this gets out of hand," Vega muttered.

Grayson blew out a slow stream of smoke. "Patience, Vega. The best show happens when you let it play out."

At the end of the dock, an orange Lexus rolled to a stop. Vaughn emerged from the shadows, his face a mask of tension and guilt. Omega stepped out of the Lexus, weary and calm, as if he had already made peace with whatever was coming.

Before he could speak, Psalm stepped forward, gun drawn.

"Time's up, Omega," she hissed. "You did good, Vaughn. Now take your sister."

Little Jewel broke free and ran to Vaughn, who scooped her up, his arms shaking. "Get in the car, Jewel," he whispered, voice cracking.

Omega exhaled, a sad smile touching his lips. "Didn't expect it to end this way." "You ain't mad?" Vaughn asked.

Omega sighed. "Because I knew my time was coming. Always did." He reached into his pocket, pulling out a set of Lexus keys. "Take 'em. It's yours now. But before I go, there's something you need to know."

Omega inhaled deeply, like a man preparing to let go of a burden he had carried for too long. His voice dropped.

"I ain't just some old head in the game, Vaughn... I'm your father."

The words slammed into Vaughn like a freight train. His pulse roared in his ears. "You're lying," Vaughn said, shaking his head.

Omega's expression remained steady. "I been watching over you your whole life. The money, the opportunities you ain't know where they came from? That was me. Always me."

Vaughn's breath hitched. "Nah... nah, this ain't real."

Omega nodded, his voice raw with regret. "I should've told you. But I was a coward."

Before Vaughn could fully process the revelation, Psalm's voice sliced through the tension. "You got my uncle killed," she spat. "And now you wanna talk about family?"

Omega exhaled. "Your uncle wasn't who you thought he was."

Psalm's hands trembled on the gun. "Shut up! You think you can rewrite the truth now?" Omega reached into his coat. "I got the paperwork."

Psalm's breath grew shallow as she scanned the documents.

"Ronnie was working with the feds, Psalm. He was a snitch."

The paper trembled in her grip. "No... he wouldn't—"

"He did." Omega's voice softened. "And you know what happens to snitches in this life." Tears burned in Psalm's eyes. Her grip on the gun slackened.

Then—slow clap ping.

A slow, deliberate clap echoed through the night, cutting through the tension like a knife. A dark chuckle followed.

Tec stepped forward from the shadows, his silhouette eerie beneath the dim glow of the harbor lights. The grin on his face was wicked, twisted with malice. Two Glocks glinted in his hands, the barrels reflecting the distant city glow.

"Well, well, well... ain't this some shit?" he drawled, shaking his head. "Ain't nothin' like a good ol' family reunion."

Vaughn stiffened, his fists clenching. "Tec. This ain't your fight."

Tec laughed, rolling his neck. "Oh, but it is. You made it my fight the moment you put that hit out on me." His eyes darkened, voice dripping venom. "But you missed... and my twin took that paid for it instead."

Vaughn's heart pounded.

Tec took a step closer, his expression contorted with grief and rage. "Blood for blood, Vaughn." His voice was low, dangerous. "You took my brother. My own flesh and blood." His hands shook slightly, but his grip on the guns never wavered. "So now I'm takin' yours."

Vaughn's breath hitched. "Tec—"

Before another word could leave his lips, two shots cracked through the night. Omega's body jerked violently as the bullets tore into his chest.

The Lexus keys slipped from his grip, clinking against the pavement.

He staggered back, his lips parting as if to say something. But no words came. Just a final exhale as his body crumpled onto the wet dock.

Vaughn's scream tore through the silence.

Then—pure chaos.

A deafening crash erupted as a storage door was kicked open. Blizz stormed in, gun blazing.

A stack of rusted buckets, piled high against the warehouse wall, toppled like an avalanche, clattering against the ground. Metal pails flew in every direction, ricocheting off crates, bouncing wildly as gunfire ripped through the dock.

One bucket smacked Tec in the head, knocking him sideways. Another spun through the air, nearly hitting Vaughn before crashing into a nearby car.

Blizz, ducking and weaving through the chaos, emptied his clip toward Tec. "I GOT YOU, BRO!" he roared, his voice wild with fury.

Tec staggered back, blood splattering across the dock, but he managed to slip into the shadows, vanishing into the night like a ghost.

The air crackled with silence.

Vaughn dropped to his knees beside Omega's lifeless body. His father.

Tears streaked his face. So many questions. No answers.

Behind him, Psalm slumped against the car, blood seeping from a wound in her side. Vaughn rushed to her, pressing his hands to her injury. "Hold on. I'm calling an ambulance." She nodded weakly, tears in her eyes. "I'm sorry, Vaughn."

He brushed her hair away from her face. "Me too."

Blizz stood nearby, his breath ragged, his eyes meeting Vaughn's.

No words passed between them. None were needed.

They stepped forward and embraced—brotherhood reforged in the ashes of betrayal.

As Blizz turned to leave, flashing lights erupted down the street.

Detectives Grayson and Vega stepped from their vehicle, eyes locked onto Blizz.

Grayson spoke into his radio. "We got him. Move in."

The night closed in, but for the first time, Vaughn felt the hint of dawn on the horizon.

CHAPTER 30: BLIZZ'S LAST RIDE

Sirens screamed through the night, their wailing cries bouncing off the towering concrete jungle. The streets pulsed with chaos, flashing red and blue lights painting the darkness in violent streaks. Blizz gripped the wheel of the stolen Charger, sweat slicking his palms as his pulse pounded in his ears.

"Breathe, Blizz. Just breathe."

The engine roared as he shot through an intersection, tires screeching in protest. The city blurred past him—neon signs, shattered glass, shadows of people diving out of the way. A squad car lunged forward, trying to cut him off. He spun the wheel hard, the Charger's rear bumper grazing the cruiser's side, sending it careening into a parked car. The impact shook the street, but Blizz didn't slow down. His eyes flicked to the rearview mirror—three more police cars swarmed behind him, their bumpers nearly kissing his own.

The radio in one of the cruisers crackled with urgency.

"Suspect is armed and dangerous! Engage with caution!"

Blizz's chest tightened. Caution was long gone. He leaned out of the driver's window, the wind whipping against his face. With one hand steady on the wheel, he lifted his gun and fired two quick shots. The first bullet shattered a windshield, forcing the officer to swerve. The second went wild. A police car skidded sideways, slamming into a streetlight. But the others pushed forward, undeterred. Blizz let off two more shots. He was going out with a bang—fuck that.

Then he heard it.

A deep whump whump whump vibrated through the air.

His stomach twisted. A helicopter. The searchlight sliced through the night, locking onto him like a hunter to its prey.

"Fuck."

Panic crawled up his spine like a frozen spider. The Charger's speedometer trembled past 100 miles per hour. The V8 engine screamed as he tore through the streets, blowing through a red light. Horns blared. A delivery truck skidded sideways, missing him by inches. His breath came in ragged gasps, his pulse thrumming in his skull.

Up ahead, an SUV barreled out of a side street. "SHIT!"
Blizz yanked the wheel. The Charger's tires shrieked. Time stretched—long enough for him to see the SUV's headlights glaring at him, the driver's panicked face frozen in terror.

Then the world exploded.

Metal crumpled. Glass shattered. The Charger flipped—once, twice—crashing down in a sickening crunch, landing upside down. Smoke billowed from the wreckage. Gasoline pooled beneath the twisted metal, the scent burning his nostrils.

Upside down. Blood trickled down his forehead. Ribs screaming. Lungs refusing to expand. Move, Blizz. Move.
With a groan, he clawed at the mangled door, kicking it open. He tumbled out, coughing, his entire body a symphony of agony. The street was a war zone—sirens, shouting, the blinding glare of headlights.

"Set up the perimeter!"

"Weapons ready!"

"He's coming out!"

Blizz stumbled to his feet, using the wreckage as cover. His fingers tightened around his gun. He checked the magazine. Only a few bullets left.

He let out a slow, trembling breath. "No regrets."
With a smirk, he pressed a crushed Percocet to his lips, letting it dissolve bitter on his tongue. His heartbeat slowed, the pain dulling.

Then—

Gunfire.

Blizz whipped around, returning fire, his arm jerking with each pull of the trigger. He fired wildly, his desperation laced in every shot.

A bullet tore through his shoulder.

"Aghhhh!" he yelled as he took cover behind the flipped Charger. The gunfire from the police seized.

Detective Grayson spoke on the bullhorn.

"Put the gun down, Blizz. You're surrounded. There's no way out."

What seemed like the entire police force had their guns trained on him, fingers hovering over triggers, waiting for a reason.

He sat back against the car, staring up at the sky—the stars flickering faintly behind the city's haze.

For the first time in a long time, he felt weightless. A tear slid down his cheek.

He closed his eyes for half a second, just enough for memories to flash—him and Vaughn as kids, laughing in the streets, chasing dreams that once felt real. Before the streets swallowed them. Before the betrayals. Before the blood.

The weight of it all sank into his bones—the choices, the pain, the people he lost and the person he became.

He looked at the gun in his lap. The barrel gleamed under the harsh lights.

"I'm sorry, Vaughn..."

His voice broke, almost lost in the sirens.

He raised the gun slowly. Not in defiance this time. Not to fight. But to finally let go.

Tears rolled freely now, streaking down his bloodied face. His hand trembled, the metal cool against his temple.

A breath in.

A whisper of peace.

Then he pulled the trigger.

The blast echoed through the street. Brain matter painted the side of the Charger. Everything went silent.

Blizz's storm ended—quiet, final, and heartbreakingly human.

CHAPTER 31: TIES THAT BREAK

The city was still soaked in chaos. The echoes of sirens faded as Detective Vega drove in silence, her hands steady, her mind razor-sharp. The glow of police lights flickered in the rearview mirror, but she had put enough distance between herself and the madness.

Omega was dead. That part of the story was over. Now, only one thing mattered—the money.

She turned off the main road, weaving through side streets until she reached a run-down apartment complex on the south side. The building was forgotten by time—cracked walls, rusted staircases, and windows covered with thick curtains that hid whatever business happened inside. This was one of Omega's safe houses, a place where money and secrets were stashed away.

Vega parked a few blocks down, not wanting to draw attention. She climbed the steps two at a time, her heartbeat steady. At the third-floor landing, she paused, glancing down the dimly lit hallway. Apartment 3B.

Omega had trusted her enough to tell her about this place. His emergency stash. His escape plan. He thought their late-night whispers and tangled sheets meant something. He thought his murmured "I love you" would bind her.

But she was never his.

She reached the door and punched in the code on the electronic lock. A faint beep, then a click. She slipped inside, locking it behind her.

The apartment was bare except for a couch, a table with a half-empty bottle of whiskey, and a few duffel bags piled in the corner. The air was thick with stale smoke and old wood.

She moved straight to the closet. This was where Omega had hidden it.

Pulling the false panel from the floor, she peeled back a layer of old carpet and pried open the wooden compartment beneath.

Her breath caught.

Stacks of cash, bundled tight. Piled like bricks. Hundreds of thousands. Maybe more. A slow smile crept across her lips. Her eyes gleamed with hunger.
This was it. Freedom.

She grabbed one of the duffel bags from the corner and began stuffing the bundles inside, the weight of her new life growing heavier with each stack. This was her way out—no more chasing ghosts through these filthy streets, no more looking over her shoulder.

She zipped the bag shut, slung it over her shoulder, and turned to leave—

"Going somewhere, Vega?"

The voice slid out of the shadows, sharp as a blade.

Her body went rigid. Her fingers clenched around the bag's handle. Slowly, she turned.

Detective Grayson leaned against the doorway, his figure cutting through the dim glow of the hallway light. His eyes glinted with cold amusement, his lips curled into a predator's smirk. His hand rested casually on his service weapon.

Vega's heart pounded against her ribs, but she forced her expression to remain cool. She arched a brow.

"Grayson," she said smoothly. "What are you doing here?"

He stepped inside, slow, deliberate. His gaze never left her.

"I should be asking you that." He nodded toward the duffel bag. "Looks heavy. What's in it?" "Evidence," she replied, her voice tight. "Omega's stash. I'm securing it before—"

He chuckled softly, cutting her off. "Come on, Vega. Let's not insult each other." His smirk widened as he studied her. "I knew about you and Omega. About your little side hustle. You thought you were the only one playing the game?"

A chill crawled up her spine.

"You don't understand," she tried.

"Oh, I understand perfectly." He took another step forward, the space between them shrinking. "You wanted out. You wanted to disappear. And you thought I wouldn't notice."

She moved to back away, but he was faster. His hand shot out, gripping her chin. His fingers pressed into her jaw, rough and possessive.

"You should've let me in," he murmured. "You should've given me what I wanted. Maybe then, this would've ended differently."

Rage flickered in her eyes. She yanked her face free, spitting venom. "You disgust me."

Grayson's smirk vanished. His face hardened.

"Yeah, well…" He exhaled, nodding slightly. "The feeling's mutual."

In one swift motion, he drew his gun.

Vega's breath caught.

"Grayson—wait!"

He shook his head slowly, almost regretfully. "Too late for that."

The gunshot ripped through the silence.

A searing pain bloomed in her chest, stealing her breath. The duffel bag slipped from her grasp, cash spilling across the floor like fallen autumn leaves.

Her knees buckled. She hit the ground hard, eyes wide, shock freezing her in place.

Grayson crouched beside her, his face inches from hers. He reached out, brushing a strand of hair from her cheek, his touch cold, almost tender.

She tried to speak. No words came.

"Should've played nice, sweetheart."

Her vision blurred. Darkness curled around the edges. Blood bubbled in her throat. Her final breath rattled out as her world collapsed into silence.

Grayson stood, slipping his gun back into his holster. He grabbed the duffel bag, hoisting it over his shoulder.

The weight felt good in his hands.

Without another glance at Vega's lifeless body, he stepped out into the night. The door swung shut behind him.

CHAPTER 32: SHADOWS OF THE PAST

The road stretched ahead, endless and empty, swallowed by the creeping dawn. Vaughn gripped the steering wheel tighter, his knuckles pale from the pressure. His chest felt heavy, but he couldn't afford to break—not now, not when she was watching.

Beside him, Little Jewel sat quietly, clutching a worn stuffed bear. The early light of morning cast a golden glow over her small face, but there was no warmth in her eyes. She had seen too much, felt too much.

Vaughn cleared his throat, forcing steadiness into his voice. "We're gonna be alright, you hear me?"

Jewel turned to him, her voice barely above a whisper. "You promise?"

"I promise," he said, firm but gentle. "No more bad nights, no more scary stuff. Just you and me. A big house in Atlanta, a yard, and a white picket fence. A real home."

She managed a small smile. "Will I have my own room?"

Vaughn chuckled, ruffling her hair. "Your own room, your own bed, and a closet full of clothes. Whatever you want."

For a moment, hope flickered in Jewel's eyes. Then, just as quickly, it faded. She looked down, voice small. "I wanna say goodbye to Mama."

Vaughn's jaw tightened. Dee Dee. The woman who should've protected Jewel. The woman who had betrayed them both. She had crossed the line when she kidnapped Jewel and handed her over to his enemies. There was no coming back from that. To him, the woman who had birthed him was already dead.

But to Jewel, she was still Mama.

Vaughn exhaled slowly, forcing himself to stay calm. "You sure?"

"She's still my mom," she whispered, her voice trembling.

Pure-hearted. Forgiving. Too good for this world.

He had no choice but to respect her wishes. With a nod, he turned onto a familiar street lined with worn-down houses and memories he wished he could bury.

Dee Dee's house sat at the end of the block, dark and lifeless. The front yard was cluttered with debris, the screen door barely hanging onto its hinges. The house was a relic of a past they were trying to outrun.

Vaughn pulled up to the curb. Jewel clutched her bear, took a shaky breath, and stepped out. He watched as her small figure disappeared through the door. The creak of its hinges echoed, then silence.

His phone buzzed. He pulled it from his pocket. "Mugz, talk to me."

Mugz's deep voice crackled through the line. "Vaughn… Psalm's in bad shape. She's in a coma. They say she's got a chance, but it's slim."

Vaughn's heart clenched. He shut his eyes, pressing a hand to his forehead. Psalm…

"Stay with her," he said hoarsely. "Don't leave her side. I don't care how long it takes. You hear me?"

"I got you, bro. I'll stay."

The line went dead. A heavy sigh escaped Vaughn's lips. Then—a scream.
Sharp. Piercing.

Jewel.

He bolted from the car, heart hammering as he ran inside. The living room smelled of decay. The air was thick, suffocating.

Jewel stood in the bedroom doorway, frozen. Tears streamed down her face. Vaughn followed her gaze—and his stomach dropped.

Dee Dee slumped against the wall, head tilted, vacant eyes staring at nothing. A syringe dangled from her limp arm. The deep tracks along her skin told a story of pain, surrender... defeat.

Vaughn moved to shield Jewel from the sight, but she clung to his leg, her body trembling. "Mama..." her voice cracked, small and broken. "Why did she...?"

Vaughn knelt, pulling her into his arms, his own chest tightening with grief. "I'm so sorry, baby. I'm so, so sorry."

Jewel buried her face in his shirt, sobbing. He held her tighter, whispering over and over, "I got you. I'll always have you."

Mugz sat slouched in the hospital chair, his elbows on his knees, eyes locked on Psalm's still body. The steady beeping of the machines filled the room, but it didn't make him feel any better. It was too quiet, too damn still.

She looked small in that bed, wires and tubes running from her like she was barely holding on. This wasn't the Psalm he knew—the one with fire in her eyes, the one who always had something smart to say.

He rubbed a hand over his face, exhaustion creeping up on him, but he wouldn't leave. Vaughn told him to stay. And he would, no matter how long it took.

Then the door creaked open.

A doctor stepped inside, dressed in a white coat, clipboard in hand. His face was neutral, calm—too calm.

"Excuse me, sir," the man said, adjusting his glasses. "We need to run a few neurological tests. I'll have to ask you to step out for a moment."

Mugz frowned, his fingers tightening around the armrests. "Tests? What kind of tests?"

The doctor's voice was smooth, controlled. "Routine brain function checks. Won't take long."

Mugz hesitated, glancing at Psalm's still form. "She don't need no damn tests, she need to wake up."

The doctor offered a small, reassuring smile behind the mask. "This will help determine how close she is to waking up."

A heavy sigh escaped Mugz. "Aight, man. Just take care of her."

He stood, rolling his shoulders, and threw one last glance at Psalm before stepping out. The door clicked shut behind him.

Silence.

Then, the doctor exhaled and rolled his neck like he had just stepped into his own home. The glasses came off, tucked into the pocket of the coat he didn't belong in. The clipboard dropped onto the counter with a careless clack.

And then he spoke—his voice lower, rougher, coated with amusement. The voice was Tec's.
"Wiggle your toes if you can hear me, ma."

For a long moment, nothing happened.

Then, just the faintest movement. A twitch beneath the sheets.

Tec smirked.

"I knew you were in there."

He sat on the edge of the bed, drumming his fingers along the mattress. "You been real quiet, huh? Playing dead? That's cute." His voice softened mockingly. "Almost had me thinking you were gone for real."

Psalm's breathing hitched, just barely, but he caught it.

His smirk widened.

He leaned in, voice dropping to a whisper, his breath warm against her ear. "You disappointed me, baby."

His fingers trailed along the IV line before gripping it loosely.

"You had one job. One. Finish off Omega. And Vaughn."

Her body remained still, but he knew she could hear him. He felt it. "But you went soft on me."

His fingers tightened around the IV line. A slow, calculated squeeze. The flow of oxygen in her bloodstream thinned.

The beeping of the machines grew erratic. The warning alarms flared.

Psalm's breath faltered. A weak, choked sound barely escaped her lips.

Tec watched her struggle, eyes dark with something unreadable. He tilted his head, watching the panic ripple through her unresponsive body, the way her chest rose in shallow, desperate gasps.

He wanted her to feel this.

"What happened, huh?" His voice was smooth, controlled. "You had the shot. You had the plan. You were supposed to be a killer, not some scared little girl."

He shook his head, clicking his tongue. "Letting Omega walk? Letting Vaughn live?" He scoffed. "That ain't you, baby. That ain't us."

He loosened his grip on the IV, allowing her breath to come easier—but only just.

He leaned closer, brushing his lips against her temple, whispering against her skin.

"I should've been enough for you."

His fingers trailed down the side of her face, slow and deliberate.

"But you just had to choose him over me, huh?"

His jaw clenched, the amusement draining from his face. "You made a fool outta me."

A cold chuckle slipped past his lips as he straightened up. He smoothed out the stolen coat, adjusting the collar like he had just finished a casual conversation.

His eyes flicked back to her, watching her fight to breathe.

"I'll let you live. For now."

His fingers brushed against her wrist one last time, his touch deceptively soft.

"But when you wake up?" He let the words hang, letting them sink into the fragile space between them.

"I'll be back. And I'll finish what you couldn't."

Then, as if nothing had happened, Tec turned on his heel and walked out of the room.

The door clicked shut behind him.

Psalm's machines beeped wildly in the background, her body still trapped in the darkness.

Vaughn tapped his fingers against the steering wheel, his eyes fixed on the road ahead. His body ached from exhaustion, but his mind wouldn't slow down. Every mile that passed, every road sign that flashed by, it all felt like he was running from something he knew would eventually catch up to him.

Beside him, Little Jewel was curled up in the passenger seat, her stuffed bear tucked tightly against her chest. She hadn't let it go once since they left the city. Every now and then, her eyelids would droop, but she fought off sleep like she was afraid of what would happen when she closed her eyes.

"We're almost there," Vaughn murmured, more to himself than to her.

Jewel turned her head, her voice barely above a whisper. "Where's there?"

Vaughn exhaled. "A fresh start."

She nodded but didn't say anything else. He knew she wanted to believe him. Hell, he wanted to believe himself.

The Georgia state line sign flashed past them, and Vaughn let out a slow breath. They had made it.

Up ahead, a red light forced him to stop at the exit ramp. The streets were quiet, nothing but the occasional car rolling by, headlights bouncing off the dark pavement. He reached for his phone, needing a distraction.

His thumb swiped over Instagram, the habit second nature. But what he saw next made his blood run cold.

Blizz.

His face was everywhere.

"RIP Blizz."

"High speed chase ended in a suicide."

"Damn Blizz you fucked the city up with this one RIP."

Vaughn's breathing stalled. His eyes flicked to a video—shaky phone footage of flashing sirens, Blizz stepping out of a car, busting his gun while taking cover ."

His stomach twisted. His hands clenched the phone so hard he thought he would crush the device into pieces.

Blizz was gone.

They hadn't spoken. Hadn't fixed things. Hadn't made things right. The light turned green. Vaughn didn't move.

Jewel shifted beside him. "Vaughn?"

He forced himself to swallow the grief clawing up his throat. He set the phone down, pressed his foot against the gas, and pulled forward.

Then, in the rearview mirror—flashing red and blue lights.

"Shit," Vaughn muttered under his breath. His stomach dropped as the sirens wailed behind him. He wasn't speeding. He hadn't run a light.
Jewel sat up, clutching her bear tighter. "What's happening?"

Vaughn pulled over to the shoulder, his heart pounding. He took a slow breath, his fingers flexing against the wheel as a stocky officer with a hard jaw and mirrored sunglasses approached his window.

Vaughn rolled it down, jaw tight. "Evening, officer."

The cop's expression was blank, cold. "License and registration." Vaughn handed them over. "Was I speeding?"
The cop ignored the question, glancing over the documents before flicking his gaze back to Vaughn. "Step out of the vehicle."

Vaughn's stomach knotted. "For what?"

The cop's tone sharpened. "Step. Out. Of. The. Vehicle."

Vaughn clenched his jaw but obeyed, keeping his movements slow, controlled. His muscles coiled tight with unease as he stood beside the car. Another officer, shorter and meaner-looking, moved toward Jewel's side.

Vaughn's instincts kicked in. "Don't touch her," he snapped.

The officer sneered. "Relax."

The first cop gestured toward the car. "We're searching the vehicle." Vaughn's breath hitched. "You got no reason to search—"
Before he could finish, the cop yanked open the door and started rifling through the back seat. Vaughn's pulse roared in his ears. Seconds later, the officer straightened up, holding a small bag of weed and a loaded gun.

Vaughn's blood ran ice-cold. What the fuck?

The cop's lip curled in satisfaction. "Well, well. What do we have here?"

Vaughn shook his head, disbelief crashing over him. "That ain't even mine. You planted that shit!"

The officer's grin widened. "You're under arrest."

"What about my sister?" Vaughn's voice cracked. "We're from out of town. She's got nobody here."

The cop didn't flinch. "Call DFCS," he said to his partner.

"No!" Vaughn's voice was raw. "You can't do this! You're violating my rights!"

The cop leaned in close, his breath hot and foul. "This is the state of Georgia, boy. We do what the fuck we want."

The cuffs snapped around Vaughn's wrists, cold metal biting into his skin. His world tilted, his vision blurring with rage and despair.

Jewel's cries pierced the air as she was pulled from the car, her small hands reaching for him. "Vaughn!" she screamed.
"I love you, Jewel!" he choked out. "I'll get you back! I promise!"

The cop shoved him toward the squad car. The door slammed shut behind him, the final nail in the coffin of his freedom.

As the car pulled away, the sun dipped below the horizon. The road ahead was dark.

And so was everything else.

To Be Continued...